Jay Quinn
Editor

Rebel Y

Stories by Cont
Southern Gay

Pre-publication
REVIEWS,
COMMENTARIES,
EVALUATIONS . . .

"**T**he South is, and always has been, the home of great fiction. *Rebel Yell* lives up to this reputation. In the best tradition of Southern writing—or any writing for that matter—each and every one of these stories casts a powerful spell. They are at times both haunting and haunted, both beautiful and brutal, as the old South, new South, and gay South meet and mingle in a narrative landscape of men, memories, and the memory of men. But more than that, *Rebel Yell* transcends its subject and setting and speaks to the rebel in us all. No doubt it will have a large audience, as do the writers it recalls."

John P. Anders, PhD
Author,
*Willa Cather's Sexual Aesthetics
and the Male Homosexual Literary Tradition*

"**Q**uinn, author of the memoir *The Mentor,* presents a superb collection of stories relating to the Southern gay experience. He has done a nice job not only of gathering these fine stories but of choosing how one flows into the next. It's rare to find a collection that doesn't contain at least a few weak selections, and this one proves to be one of those exceptions. The book is recommended for several reasons. First, it is an excellent selection of stories. Second, voices from the South and from rural areas are absent in most gay literature collections. And third, these authors have something important to say. How often does that happen?"

Library Journal

More pre-publication
REVIEWS, COMMENTARIES, EVALUATIONS . . .

"**A**merica's gay community extends far beyond the gay Meccas of LA's West Hollywood, New York's West Village, and San Francisco's Castro District to all sections of the USA. Attention in the gay media and literature is focused on the major centers of gay life in California and on the East Coast, stretching no further south than Washington, DC. Quinn's anthology of fourteen Southern stories written by contemporary gay men savors the heritage of what it means to be gay and Southern, both in terms of contradiction and complement.

The narratives study aspects of life, be it family of origin, childhood experiences, Southern worldview, and often a combination of all three. Their sexual orientation is just one of the many facets of gay men that are explored. The stories serve at times as celebrations and at times critiques of what it means to be Southern and gay.

Coming-out experiences (as youth and adults); regional tradition; Southern sensibilities; AIDS; and the impact of religion, education, and family values on the authors are all explored. Accounts flow with a journey through each author's roots and sexuality; how they intertwine captivates the reader.

This collection is expertly crafted, being pragmatic and determined while remaining distinctively Southern. The stories are poignant, witty, and proud. It is a recommended read for gay adults and gay high school students and also for parents (especially those from the South) coming to terms with their gay sons' sexual orientation."

John R. Selig
ForeWord Magazine

"**G**ay boys from the South may be pretty and sweet, but what about their lives? The writers in this collection give you a peek at theirs, in voices as familiar as your best friend's. Bullies, hunks, and lovers pull at our sleeves, taking us down old country roads and even older memories. But combustive winds blow through the Southern culture, igniting trouble and sending boys running off to the far boundaries of experience.

That is what makes up the soul of *Rebel Yell*. These are the songs of outcasts. Full of punch and nostalgia, their stories validate our own lives. Here are the men who finally leave their mothers for long-ago lovers, the boys who are as-comfortably-as-they-can-be gay, and the other kids, the ones who are bludgeoned halfway to martyrdom. The fourteen talented writers in this collection have contributed poignantly to the literature of gay existence in the contemporary South."

Walter A. de Milly, III
Author,
In My Father's Arms:
A True Story of Incest

❧

"**F**rom lighthearted to gothic to downright creepy, *Rebel Yell* is a richly insightful and unsettling portrait of American Life."

Will Fellows
Author,
Farmboys: Lives of Gay Men
from the Rural Midwest

More pre-publication
REVIEWS, COMMENTARIES, EVALUATIONS . . .

"*Rebel Yell* joins *Bastard Out of Carolina, All Over but the Shoutin',* and *The Liar's Club* on my short list of books that honestly capture the atmosphere, both positive and negative, of the South I know, the South I love and fear simultaneously. This collection captures, in its mix of haunting fiction and frightening reality, the atmosphere in which Southern gay men live.

Like the first published coming-out stories, so necessary for gay men and lesbians in forming a positive sense of self, the stories in *Rebel Yell* provide, perhaps for the first time, the stories of Southern gay men living at the nexus of racism, classism, and misogyny that is, unfortunately, at the heart of Southern experience. These pieces, written by the queer sons of the country's queerest region, provide a missing piece in the puzzle of Southern experience.

Reading *Rebel Yell* is like attending a queer class reunion in my small Southern hometown. These are voices of the friends/compatriots/mentors/lovers I longed for growing up gay in the South. The positive difference reading these stories and recognizing my adolescent self in them would have made to me as a young man is immeasurable. Young Southern gay men today are lucky to have such a book available to them."

Carlos L. Dews, PhD
Editor, *This Fine Place So Far from Home: Voices of Academics from the Working Class; Out in the South;* and *Illumination and Night Glare: The Unfinished Autobiography of Carson McCullers*

"There's much more to *Rebel Yell* than grits and humidity, chewin' tobacco, and repressive religion. There is also an 'otherness' that sets these stories—of first sex, impossible love, parental shock, impenetrable ignorance, essential sweetness, fumbling coming out, fierce determination to be true to oneself—apart from the bicoastal triangle of NY/LA/SF fiction and memoir. The situations are universal, the rites of pain all too common among gay men everywhere in America; but these shared stories are told by discernibly different voices, telling of a world of different manners and morality, of unique expectation and inherited style."

Richard Labonte
Former General Manager,
A Different Light Bookstores;
Book Columnist,
www.planetout.com
and www.contentville.com

Rebel Yell
Stories by Contemporary Southern Gay Authors

HARRINGTON PARK PRESS
Southern Tier Editions
Gay Men's Fiction
Jay Quinn, Executive Editor

Love, the Magician by Brian Bouldrey

Distortion by Stephen Beachy

The City Kid by Paul Reidinger

Rebel Yell: Stories by Contemporary Southern Gay Authors edited by Jay Quinn

Rebel Yell
Stories by Contemporary Southern Gay Authors

Jay Quinn
Editor

HPP

Southern Tier Editions
Harrington Park Press®
An Imprint of The Haworth Press, Inc.
New York • London • Oxford

Published by

Southern Tier Editions, Harrington Park Press®, an imprint of The Haworth Press, Inc., 10 Alice Street, Binghamton, NY 13904-1580.

PUBLISHER'S NOTE
This is a work of fiction. Names, characters, places, and incidents either are the products of the author's imagination or are used fictitiously, and any resemblance to actual persons, living or dead, business establishments, events, or locales is entirely coincidental.

Cover design by Marylouise E. Doyle.

Library of Congress Cataloging-in-Publication Data

Rebel yell : stories by contemporary southern gay authors / Jay Quinn, editor.
    p. cm.
    ISBN 1-56023-160-2—ISBN 1-56023-161-0 (pbk.)
    1. Gay men's writings, American. 2. Short stories, American—Southern States. 3. Gay men—Fiction. 4. American fiction—20th century. 5. American Fiction—Southern States. 6. Southern States—Social life and customs—Fiction. I. Quinn, Jay.

PS647.G39 R43 2000
813'.018920642'09045—dc21
                                     00-063370

There ain't no way to make it perfect.

You do the best you can for the people left, a yard-fighting, teeth-gnashing, biscuit-eating, ugly-dog-raising, towel-stealing, television praying, never-forgiving, hard-headed people that you love with all the strength in your body, once you finally figure out that they are who you are, and, in many ways, all there is.

Rick Bragg
All Over but the Shoutin'

CONTENTS

Preface

All I have to do is open my mouth. I speak, and anyone will know two things about me: I'm Southern and I'm gay. Despite more years of Marlboros than I like to acknowledge, my voice still has an unmistakable gay lilt, though registering on the low, gritty end of that scale. My life path has taken me from a dirt road in eastern North Carolina, to Paris, to Manhattan, to Guam, and a lot of spots and places in between. Still, the singular patois of spoken black and Southern English asserts itself. "Mouth" becomes "mowf." "Right" becomes "roight." "Boiled" becomes "bald." Undeniably, this is my voice. This is who I am. That is where I'm from.

In the current, relentless, postmodernist deconstruction of identity and intent, what does my stubborn accent's disingenuous revelation reveal? I think it most strongly proves a visceral memory of place, of time and of continuity in an increasingly alien, yet homogenized, world.

It appears to me that our broad-brushed rush to embrace diversity results in either the muting of all the hues of individuality to a toneless pattern of grays, or a hysterical amplification of the most minute aspects of that individuality. I think of a child playing with the contrast controls of a television set, fascinated by the reduction of color to black and white and the blossoming of gray to Technicolor, settling finally for the fullness of the balanced spectrum.

Gay men possess just such experience in their views of the world. The vivid hues of childhood become telescoped and transmuted into a colorless landscape with their growing perception of themselves as "other" in a milieu dominated by a heterosexual hegemony. With their assertion of self, nudged and strengthened by the twin drives of desire and desolation, they experience a rapid intensification of value and color in their lives, as they seek and find community and love beyond an atonal landscape of conformity and constriction. Experience, heartbreak, and happiness all serve to return them to a liveable middle range in the spectrum of their lives.

The reconciliation of color and black and white brings a fuller understanding and appreciation of one's heritage and home. Dancing in the splintered light of a mirror ball can still evoke the endless scattering of stars across a blue-black summer night sky. While home can be conjured by the sharp, nasal twang of my Yankee partner's New Jersey voice, it can still be evoked by the passing sibilance of a stranger's unmistakable Down East brogue. It is my spectrum, the one that reaches out from me to the past, to the future, placing me in my now.

My now is outside of the South. The part of Florida where I live isn't southern; it's New York's backyard and the Caribbean's capitol. The South I know, that honeyed accumulation of humidity, old hatred, enduring ignorance, and surprising sweetness, really exists only in me. Filtered through my gay eyes and revealed in my gay voice, it is portable, and it endures beyond the cartoonish, condescending characterization perpetrated on it by the rest of the nation and the world.

When I found the middle of my own spectrum of color and embraced my identity as both a Southerner and a gay man, I found one had aided and enhanced the other. From my Southern heritage of stubborn loyalty, arrogance, and resentment, I had crafted my identity as a pragmatic and determined gay man.

That same redneck truculence that precedes my notions of self-worth and honor allows me to say, "You can kiss my ass," both to those who make fun of my accent and to the host of fundamentalist Christians who despise my gayness. A product of the rigid class system yet undead in the South, I can cry when Travis Tritt sings, "I'm gonna be somebody. One of these days I'm gonna break these chains." Because I can cry when I hear that song or when Old Yeller dies, my sentiment informs my tenderness. And because I heard hellfire and brimstone preaching on many hot summer nights, I can enjoy the burn of hard liquor and fuck your brains out knowing both the risk of damnation and the sweetness of redemption.

It is those very conundrums that have elevated the Southern gay male from cartoon to erotic icon in the canon of not only gay literature but American literature as well. It is a small step from Herman Wouk's Youngblood Hawke in the same-titled book to Carl Corley's gay pulp hero, Cutty Ragan, of *A Fool's Advice,* to Felice Picano's Pensacola Rick in *Like People in History,* to Tony Blair in Paul Russell's *Boys of Life.* Each author's rangy, drawling, sleepy-eyed good ol' boy personifies a blend of raw-boned sensuality and menace uniquely Southern in context and action. But that is not all we are. More than well-hung naïfs or cunning country bumpkins, we are real men. We exist in every color beyond an eroticized, unnuanced black and white.

At the urging of Bill Cohen, publisher of The Haworth Press, I undertook the search for contemporary Southern gay stories, from contemporary Southern gay writers, to see what had endured of the icon and the identity. The contemporary South is now home as much to hi-tech carpetbaggers and real estate developers as it is to crackers and broken-down aristocracy. I wanted to see where the identities of today's Southern gay men fell in the same spectrum that includes AIDS and Jerry Falwell; MTV and Grand Ole Opry; stump liquor and chardonnay; David Duke and John Berendt.

The efforts of the following fourteen contributors are the results of that search. In their voices, I hear the familiar cadences of drawl and twang. In their stories, I find the enduring contradiction and complement in what it means to be both Southern and gay today. Undeniably, these are our voices. This is who we are. This is where we're from.

Stubborn, beaten and victorious, sentimental and sensual, proud— we add our voices to that historic shout uttered in the face of bullets or broken Budweiser bottles and at those who would seek to cast us as a caricature or cartoon. It's our Rebel Yell.

Jay Quinn
Ft. Lauderdale

Acknowledgments

The undertaking of any work of words is only possible with the support, collusion, and constant nurture of key individuals. Their invaluable part in the realization of this work is gratefully recognized in this too meager mention for their role. At The Haworth Press: Bill Cohen, Bill Palmer, Amy Rentner, Peg Marr; in the world of words: Shelley Bindon, Tom Long, Paul Lisicky, Nicholas Weinstock; in the world of work: Anita Landis, Dale Baron, Anne Grigsby; in hand and heart, Susan Highsmith, Debi Brown, Joe Riddick; and always and in every way: Jeff Auchter.

In 1974, a skinny, too-pretty white boy in eastern North Carolina read *I Know Why the Caged Bird Sings.* Maya Angelou taught him that a common history of anger, pain, love, and dreams could fit your feet to the dirt road out of bigotry, ignorance, and oppression. She gave him a way to speak.

I hope I've honored that gift by passing it on. I dedicate this book to her.

The Wilds

Robin Lippincott

I had just turned sixteen, that heartbreaking spring of 1974, when Colin died. We had met two years earlier in an eighth-grade art class; Colin had been sent to live with his grandparents, two sad, lost ex-Dubliners in their midsixties whose much loved son had been killed (decapitated) in a horrendous automobile accident. The Welch's seemed baffled, slightly resentful even, that this teenage boy who looked so much like their very own Paddy should become their charge and serve as a daily reminder of his loss, but there was no one else for Colin after his mother, Rosa—a tiny Sicilian rendered literally speechless by the trauma of her husband's sudden death—was hospitalized for the third time that year. So Colin came to St. Mark's, a small town on Florida's Gulf Coast not far west of Tallahassee, where I live now.

I was then a lonely and romantic boy, the only child of two well-meaning people who, although still in their late forties, were already worn down and defeated. It was easy to see why, since daily life was uneventful and dull. I longed for drama and meaning, and for otherness.

Colin made a quick impression—mop of mussed and wavy black hair, flashing green eyes, generous mouth; his skin was the palest I had ever seen: he was extremely sensitive to the sun. Colin wore a black turtleneck that first day, an article of clothing that was new to me, and I learned he was from Boston.

Clearly, I was primed for Colin's friendship, and he, a virtual orphan, was equally ripe for mine—a boy made so terribly vulnerable by the death of his father, the absence of his mother, and what appeared to me to be the indifference of his grandparents.

It must have been about a week after he first walked into the classroom that we ran into each other on the way home from school.

"I'm Colin," he said. He had a slight Boston accent, though none of its ugly harshness.

"Rupert," I responded, hands shoved deep into my pockets—my self-protective, tough-guy stance.

"So what do you do for a good time around here?" Colin asked as we walked along the dirt road in front of the school.

I shrugged. "We don't," I said, and he laughed. He looked at me for a few seconds, then asked if I had lived here all my life. When I nodded, he just shook his head and looked around.

"Man!" he sighed.

I thought this an appropriate-enough response. "Yeah," I added.

"Man!" Colin repeated, his entire body shaking. "I've got the wilds so bad."

"The what?"

"Oh," he recovered, as if only then realizing where he was, whom he was with. "That's something my Dad used to say a lot; I think it's Irish or something—he was Irish. It means, like, I don't know—like a crazy, restless sort of feeling."

"I've had that feeling all my life," I told him, not smiling.

"He's dead," Colin added, as if in a trance. "My dad." Then he proceeded to tell me the bare bones of his story—all very brief and without emotion.

When he finished, I didn't know what to say—I felt overwhelmed. We continued to walk along in silence, heads down, kicking at the dirt road. And while part of my mind remained there, with Colin, in the moment, another part was already thinking about how much I liked him. "I've always wanted to go to Boston," I said. It was true.

He looked up and brightened. "Boston's cool! I mean, the city's so old, you know? Just about everything has a history and *means* something. Not like here," he added under his breath, looking around. "And there's always stuff to do, like riding the subway, or seeing all the hippies in Harvard Square, or ice skating . . ."

But at about that point, I tuned out—something that happened to me a lot back then. It seemed that whenever anything really good was going on, or whenever I felt particularly excited, probably *because* it wasn't often, I couldn't take too much at once. I had to step back, to stash it, store it away—temporarily. Then, as soon as I could, I would rush home. There, safe in my room, I would unpack the memory and pour over it, savor it—rehashing, rubbing, cherishing.

"I guess I should be going," I said to Colin, looking up. For a moment, everything appeared unfamiliar and I didn't know where I was. We were still on the road in front of the school that I had walked countless times, but I had been transported.

"Yeah, me too," he said, eyeing me. Establishing that we lived only a few blocks from each other, and because the following day was a Saturday, we agreed to meet in front of the school at noon.

Before long, Colin and I were spending practically all of our free time together. Clearly, I was in love almost from the start, and just as clearly (in retrospect), Colin was not—neither immediately nor later—but for awhile he either thought or tried to pretend that he was. And because I was in love with him and desperately wanted his love in return, I probably pushed him to think that he did love me; for awhile I think we both believed it.

Our favorite hangout was the St. Mark's Lighthouse, a place I had come to take for granted as part of the local landscape, until Colin came along. He was the one to discover it first, without me. He told me he *loved* lighthouses—they were all over New England. He figured he'd seen about twenty so far in his life (he was counting). And when he found out the builder of this one was from Boston, it was as if Colin had fallen in love.

"Winslow Lewis," he announced. We were there, at the lighthouse. "Built in 1829. Made of limestone blocks." He was walking in circles around the base, trailing one hand along the lighthouse wall as he went. "I've been reading up on it. It's eighty feet high and can be seen from fifteen miles away." We looked up. "And the reflector lens is from Paris!" Typical Colin—find out everything you can about what you're interested in. For me, that something was Colin.

The lighthouse was maybe three miles from our neighborhood, and we took to riding our bikes there at all hours, though mostly at night. Colin could come and go as he pleased, and I could always effectively sneak out my bedroom window. On one of our earliest visits, we were just sitting there, looking out at the ocean at twilight, when Colin mentioned his mother. It was completely offhand and anecdotal, but because it was the only time he ever did so, I remember it vividly. She had a small dog (he said this as if it were her dog alone and not the family dog); he didn't tell me its name. Mornings, he said, as his mother was making her first cup of espresso, the dog would dance around her legs and yap until she made a cup *for him* as well, which she always did— and which, according to Colin, the little dog immediately lapped up. That was it. I laughed at the oddness of it, and Colin laughed a little, too. Whatever else the story meant to him or what I was supposed to glean from it, if anything, I can't say.

He spoke of his father more often; for example, Colin told me that he was a carpenter and had incredible hands, and that he played hockey and told stories. But usually Colin mentioned his father only to attribute something to him—a word, a phrase, or a way of doing things. It was clear that Colin came from a unique family, and just as clear that they meant a great deal to him, despite his reluctance to show it. For now, Colin seemed a boy without a past; he was, at that point and for awhile, the most present, in-the-moment person I have ever met, and yet even the present did not satisfy him. He was constantly moving about, talking, smoking, planning—always seemingly ill at ease, projecting into the future. I guess that was his legacy. In the two years that I knew him, I saw Colin go from a healthy, normal-looking boy to a tormented and wasted ghoul.

The first time we were at the lighthouse at night it was after midnight, school was out for the summer, and a fierce thunderstorm was fast approaching—I could see heat lightning flashing on the horizon; just riding our bikes there, against the strong wind, had been an ordeal. The place had an otherworldly, desolate feel to it. Every grain of sand, it seemed, had been blown off the concrete base; waves broke on the shore, and the oleander bushes surrounding the lighthouse, with their sweet-smelling pink blossoms, rustled in the wind. But there was the revolving beam of the lighthouse, flooding us with light, then sweeping off and plunging us into darkness. Piercing light, then pitch darkness— again and again—a slow strobe. I was already a reader of poetry then, and so it seemed only natural that these lines should come to me (I recited them aloud):

> "And we are here as on a darkling plain
> Swept with confused alarms of struggle and flight
> Where ignorant armies clash by night."

"What's that?" Colin asked, shouting above the wind and the surf.

I could tell he liked it, was interested. "It's from a poem called 'Dover Beach.'"

"Cool!" was Colin's response.

The approaching storm, the regular, pulsing flash of the lighthouse beacon showed Colin there, then gone, there again, but in a different position. We circled the lighthouse, continuing to talk. Then, in the darkness, we ran into each other. Colin had reversed his direction without telling me. The light flooded us, and for a moment, there he was—eyes, nose, mouth—mere inches in front of me—electric! So close that I could feel and smell his breath (cigarettes), in one of the intervals of darkness, Colin embraced me, quickly and hard, then he let go and proceeded to circle. My knees were shaky and I could still feel the imprint of his embrace—his arms locked together just beneath my shoulder blades; his chest pressing hard against mine; the left side of his face brushing against my left cheek; a lock of his hair caught in my eyelashes. I was delirious. And yet after the initial rush of pleasure, something else, a kind of discomfort, began to creep into my consciousness, too. That something, I believe now, was the clinging desperation I liken—these many years and experiences later—to that of throwing oneself against a stranger, as if to say, "Save me!"—something I have done often in the years since Colin's death.

"Let's lie down and look up at it," Colin suggested, gesturing toward the lighthouse. We did so, head to head, then looked up at the now-foreshortened towering base to the attention-grabbing beacon as it revolved around and around, spreading its fingers of light.

I reached back and took one of Colin's hands in mine, and he let me have it.

"Let's call this place 'The Wilds,'" he said.

I squeezed his hand briefly and said okay, then let go; I'd had an idea. I sat up. "But we should have some sort of a ceremony, you know, like a christening or something."

That was all I needed to say. Colin was already taking off his clothes. I followed suit, more slowly since I was watching him, and I quickly discovered that he wore no underwear—another *first,* for me. Then, there, quite suddenly and unexpectedly, Colin was completely naked. To say that his body was beautiful, or that the sight of him took my breath away, sounds banal, and yet both are true. The perfect David who stood before me was just that—a true specimen of young manhood. I had my pants and underwear still to go but now tore them off. Quickly we took off running in the direction of the ocean until we could run no more, until the height and weight and volume of the water combined to stop and swallow us. After completely immersing himself, Colin seemed to shoot up out of the sea and into the night sky, screaming and yelping and yahooing and splashing about; but once again, there seemed to be a desperation to it—at least that is what I see now.

After eight months' time, I began to see that Colin was slowly unraveling, not that he talked about it—though he did tell me he was having difficulty sleeping. I could see with my own eyes that he was losing weight. I didn't know what to do, how to save him, but it was to that end, spending the weekend at his house while his grandparents were back in Dublin visiting relatives, that I told him I loved him. We had become demonstrative in our affection for each other by this point, hugging with every greeting and leave-taking (outside of school), but neither of us had ventured so far as to express his feelings verbally.

We were sitting on the living room sofa, eating spaghetti; the TV was on.

"I love you, too," he responded, very matter of factly, his voice as flat as the EKG of a dead man.

I looked at him. His eyes were blank, reflecting the television screen.

"I want you to fuck me," I said suddenly, harsh, because Colin always harped on our need to toughen up. I thought he would like it. The words simply popped out, unexpected, even though I'd been thinking not only of saying it but also how I would say it for quite some time. It was something I wanted to give to Colin, and something I wanted to do to myself, to experience. I knew it would hurt. The time seemed right.

At first he was silent. The TV droned in the background. "Have you ever done it before?" he finally asked.

Perhaps I should have known it was a mistake when Colin couldn't, or wouldn't, look me in the eyes. But I was lost; I shook my head. "You?"

He nodded. "Once, in Boston. With a girl."

He took me by the hand and led me into his bedroom. We both began taking off our clothes. He started kissing me with his tongue: this was new and seemed to cause the room to spin. Then things began to happen very fast—we fell into bed and Colin immediately turned me over onto my stomach. I felt his erection flapping against me; he spat into his hand and began lubricating his penis. And then, slowly, he tried to enter me. I cried out in pain. I told him it hurt, but he just said "Shh," and "Shh," and ran his fingers through my hair as he pushed and rotated, gently, until he was inside me. At first he was sitting up as he began to move in and out of me, so that the image of a man riding a bronco formed in my mind; then he leaned over and resumed kissing me, and I turned my head to meet him, to receive his tongue and to give him mine. Now he began pushing harder and deeper, and I was crying out, telling him that it hurt and that I wanted him to stop. But he was at that point—of desperate momentum, of no return—where he couldn't stop, so he pressed on, and soon, finally, with the pain came pleasure, too, and I felt both a great and powerful emptying and an expansive fullness at the same time. I shuddered, and then Colin came, in repeated and seemingly endless gasps. Now there was calm, and Colin's hands encircled my torso as he rested the full weight of his body on mine for what seemed a delicious forever; it was the stillest I had ever seen him. We fell asleep that way.

From then on, Colin and I began to fuck as often as we could, but it was always just that, *fucking,* and nothing else—no foreplay, no tenderness, nothing—and he was always in the dominant position. Over time he became more callous, brutal even—as if he were trying to exorcise something. I tried to believe it didn't have anything to do with me and just be grateful for the contact.

What turned out to be the last year of Colin's life was pretty much hell, for him and for me; he seemed to be disappearing before my very eyes, and I felt powerless to help him. Where the adults were— his grandparents and teachers—and what they were thinking, *if* they were thinking much about him at all, I can't say. Because he was able to sleep so infrequently now, Colin's eyes were ringed with purply-black shadows; he told me his nights were haunted by images of his father's body, walking about headless, or the head would appear alone, bodiless. Colin had lost so much weight by this point— because he was smoking two packs of cigarettes a day and hardly eating—that his clothes appeared to be hanging on a frame. He had begun to skip school frequently, too, and sometimes, more often than not, I joined him—just to be with him and to do whatever I could to try to save him from himself. But far worse and more ominous was the fact that Colin had begun to cut at himself with whatever sharp object happened to be at hand, and to apply lit cigarettes to his skin, which had become, overall, coarse and rough to the touch. He also grew even more jittery, his nerves on edge, frayed, and we began to fight a lot. About? About nothing, or about fucking—the fact that we were, and that I was not a girl?—or simply because it wasn't helping him? I could only guess. Colin wasn't saying. Once, I took him by the shoulders and stood with him only inches in front of me, and then, holding his face in my hands, I looked into his eyes and said, "I love you, I love you," over and over again until he averted his gaze, at which point I started crying. I was so naive. I was fifteen—I just didn't have the experience.

Amidst all of this, my parents seemed to think I was becoming a juvenile delinquent and that there was nothing they could do to stop it. This, of course, was communicated primarily through glances and gestures: whereas most of my teenage years up until this time had been spent alone in my room, now I was rarely at home; therefore, didn't it follow that I must be up to no good? Very little was said, however; instead, as with most everything else in their lives, they simply resigned themselves to it. I let them down, too.

So Colin and I were all we had, and we continued to spend all of our time together, and to go to the lighthouse; we made love there, too—on the concrete base, on the beach. In fact, making love was something I had begun to use as a sort of weapon, a quick snap of the fingers, a way to bring Colin back into the moment, to give him peace, for those few, brief minutes. All I had to do was look at him and say, "Fuck me," and he always seemed to want to, perhaps because it was one of the rare opportunities in which he could lose himself.

During those last six months, Colin's bad case of the wilds expressed itself in bigger and more dramatic ways; he was always on the move— and I was almost always at his side. We jumped a boxcar, a dream of Colin's, and rode all the way to Jacksonville, sharing the train car with a couple of friendly alcoholics and a sad, homeless fourteen-year-old girl and her baby. We thumbed to Atlanta one weekend—an experience in and of itself since one of our rides, a guy wearing a yellowing priest's collar, tried to lose me and to rape Colin—a long story. Fortunately, we escaped, taking the guy's wallet and $47 in cash with us. We spent Saturday night—and the $47—in The Underground, with Colin drunk out of his mind and me just trying to stay awake and keep him out of trouble. Back in St. Mark's we did things like steal a sailboat and spend the dark hours of the night trying to navigate the rough waters of the gulf. Another one of Colin's quixotic ideas was for us to run away to Boston together; he would mention the fact that his father was buried there and that he had never seen where. And though going to Boston with Colin was something I would have wanted to do, and done, only months earlier, now, because of his swift unraveling, the idea merely frightened me.

It was as if Colin were possessed. His hair had grown wild and unruly. He looked, sometimes acted, like a madman. I tried to talk to him, to reason with him: "Where do you think all this is going?" I asked softly. "Don't you think we should try to get you some help?"

He merely shrugged.

"I'm worried about you."

This last expression of concern Colin seemed to translate as "Fuck me!" and he began grabbing at my clothes.

But sometimes now, when I was able to, I resisted. Instead, I prepared meals for him. Usually, he wouldn't touch the food, but once or twice he picked up whatever it was and crammed large portions of it into his mouth with both hands, like a savage, until there was nothing left.

We went to the lighthouse exclusively at night now; in fact, Colin scarcely went out in daylight anymore (he said it hurt his eyes). He had stopped going to school entirely by this point.

"What is it?" I asked him one night.

"What's what?"

"What's wrong?" I asked. "Can you tell me? Put it into words?"

Another shrug.

"I mean, I know about your dad and your mom and everything, Colin, but . . ."

"But what?" he flared.

I didn't have an answer. I couldn't exactly say, "But you've got to get on with your life."

So I started thinking about telling somebody, talking to somebody, asking for help. But who? I rejected our teachers out of hand. Who else? Colin's grandparents? They wouldn't get it, nor was I convinced that they cared. My parents? No. A stranger—I decided on a stranger. One night I looked in the Yellow Pages and found a number for The Samaritans. I dialed the number so many times that night, a night I had decided to try to stay away from Colin, thinking *that* might somehow bring him around. But just as many times I hung up without saying anything. What could I say? That I was worried about a friend? That he was acting funny? No, I couldn't do it; it felt like a betrayal.

Nor could I stay away from Colin. The very next night we were back at the lighthouse again. Walking on the base, circling the parameter, Colin spoke: "This is just like life, you know?" He paused as if waiting for a response. "You walk in circles, and then you die."

I groaned, stopped circling, and Colin ran into me from behind. He wrapped his arms around my chest and rested his head on my shoulder, his bony embrace sadly evoking the perfect David who was no more. I felt such a sense of loss, so desolate. I wanted the lighthouse to go dark then, to shut down and leave us in velvet blackness; I thought it would be a relief. We stood like that for a long time, until I became aware of the whistling of the wind. Then, suddenly, after an explosive crack of thunder, it began pouring rain. Colin only tightened his hold at first, then turned me around and stuck his tongue in my mouth. Before long I actually started laughing—because of the drops of rain sliding down my face and into my mouth, joined to Colin's, I was practically drowning.

He let me go and pushed his soaking hair back with his hands. "And here we are . . ." he recited, looking at me for help.

I didn't get it at first, though the insistent thrumming in his voice made me nervous. I thought he was mad at me for laughing.

"And here we are . . ." he repeated more urgently. "You know, that poem."

"Oh yeah." I was pleased that he remembered. "And we are here as on a darkling plain/Swept with confused alarms of struggle and flight/ Where ignorant armies clash by night."

"Yeah," he said, looking around, his entire body beginning to shake. "That's us—confused on a darkling plain." He gestured toward the town: "Ignorant armies." Then he sat down, and, as usual, I followed his lead.

We were quiet again for a few minutes, until Colin, eerily, ghostily—as if something had passed through him—a sea change—said, "I feel like my Dad's here. I felt it from the very beginning, the first time I came here."

I didn't know what to say. I looked around, half expecting to see Mr. Welch myself—such was Colin's power.

Colin started to weep. "I can't do this anymore," he cried, shivering. He didn't have to tell me what "this" was; the slight movement of his head in my direction that I detected said it all. I thought he meant us.

"Okay," I whispered, not looking up at him.

"No," he said. "You don't understand. No. I want . . ." He was sobbing heavily now. "I want to be with my dad." And then, without warning, he began grabbing at the pink oleander blossoms, violently tearing them from their stems and shoving them in his mouth.

I gasped because I knew, immediately, that Colin would know what he was doing, would know that *anything* from the oleander bush— flowers, leaves—was poisonous. He was chewing the flowers now, his face a fist of agony.

At first I froze: all I could think about was how bitter the flowers must taste. Then I came to and grabbed at Colin's hands: if only I could just hold them long enough to get my fingers down his throat and force him to vomit. But Colin's will was powerful and he pushed me away, so hard, in fact, that I fell off the base. I scrambled back up again, when, suddenly, a bolt of lightning illuminated the scene, and I watched, horrified, until I had to turn away. Now it was as if the flowers were being forced down my throat, too, since when I tried to speak—to scream, to call out Colin's name, to tell him to stop, to tell him that I loved him, that there were reasons to live—nothing came out. I could scarcely breathe; I was gasping for breath.

And all the while, life just went on—the rain continued to fall, more lightly now; the waves came in and went out again; the beacon of the lighthouse continued its goddamn, constant flashing. . . . And Colin continued to eat the oleander flowers.

I was crying now, too, and for a moment I just sat there in the sand, focused on the snot hanging from Colin's nose, momentarily caught in the light, as he was coughing and choking. Then I did the only other thing I knew to do, I started screaming for help, which felt so lonely and lost and futile, like casting a tiny pebble into the ocean and hoping for a big splash. I took off running for my bike, hoping that someone, anyone, might be in the area that late at night, something Colin and I had *never* wanted. I picked up my bike and climbed onto the wet seat, then paused. I looked over at Colin: his hair was in his face and his wet clothes clung to his body, which now appeared as white and lifeless as the lighthouse itself. I didn't want to leave him. The pull was so strong. But I knew I had to. I got a rush of adrenaline and took off. I was still crying, shaking, and trying to scream for help, attempting to wave one hand as I rode, but the wind and rain lashed against me, making balance precarious.

I don't know how long or how far I rode before finding another human being—an old man in a truck—it might have been only a mile or two—but by the time I told him what was happening and we threw my bike into the back, sped to the lighthouse, reached Colin, picked him up, put him in the truck, and rushed to the hospital, it was too late. Colin was dead; he had asphyxiated.

That was twenty-five years ago, and my life has gone on, or it hasn't—I'm not always sure which. But what I do know is that back then, at fourteen, when I told Colin I'd had the wilds all my life, I didn't know what I was talking about. Only now would that be true; it is Colin's legacy to me.

−2−

Fraternity:
Church, Trucks, and Men

John Trumbo

The time-honored, familial society among men of the South even today in the twenty-first century isn't easily penetrated by open homosexuality. Even though as gay men we may be born into this society, it's typically soon made clear that we're not a true member of the intended clan. Maybe that's what my dad's brother meant, consciously or subconsciously, when he told me I didn't look like I was from his side of the family. He said, in a not-too-flattering tone, that I looked like I came from my mom's family.

Later, as a boy, I was in a department store once and asked a saleslady where the bathroom was. She answered, stumbling over her words, "Honey, do you mean the little boys' room or the little girls' room?" I don't know how she, too, knew that I was from my mom's side of the family, but I became more determined than ever to grow up to be a man—to walk with a self-assured swagger, speak deeply and slowly, shake hands firmly, slap backs, and shoot the shit. But I don't remember the moment when I received my official initiation into the society of men.

The society of men was perhaps most present and most daunting in my family's Southern Baptist Church. If you're picturing a little white country church (white being not just the color of the paint on the outside) that might adorn a snowy Christmas card, you've got it right. The church sat across from the volunteer fire department, and often when the fire alarm would sound during a sermon, our pastor would have to pause because the noise drowned out even him. I watched with great admiration as several men in the congregation quietly but hurriedly left their families sitting in their pews and rushed out to attend to the emergency.

I was ten or eleven when I was baptized there. I accepted the Lord during a summer revival. It wasn't the sweltering come-to-meeting-style revival held in a tent, like many in the South, but it was hot and inspiring nonetheless. I believe I was sitting with friends, not my family, when the call came from Above. A lot of other folks were responding to the pastor's invitation, and it seemed only natural that I join them. I crawled over my friends' legs, many of them nodding off or drawing, and found my way to the front. "I want to be saved," I said when I got there. It was a moment I had been raised to anticipate, like getting married, but it was startling when it finally arrived.

On the long-awaited day of my baptism (events like this are planned well in advance for Southern Baptists), my dad led me into a room with all the other men waiting to be baptized so we could change into our gowns. As I started taking off my clothes to prepare to enter the heavenly family, I suddenly felt very conspicuous. I wasn't ashamed of anything I had done, not that I can remember. I was just ashamed of being naked in church in front of a bunch of other men. I wanted to stop; I didn't want to be saved that day. I wept. My dad, probably having no idea what I was doing, kept helping me with my clothes, absent-mindedly ignoring my tears and fears.

Moving out into the foyer beside the choir loft where the baptismal pool was, I found some relief from my emotions in the silence of the service. My stomach was still in knots, however, as I stared down at the plastic carpet runner beneath my bare feet, its dozens of little plastic teeth biting into the carpet it was protecting.

At some point, it became my turn to climb the choir loft steps. As I did, our friendly old pastor was waiting for me in the water with his arms outstretched, a big smile on his wrinkled face. I knew him. He comforted me. At that point, he was the only person present. He embraced me, whispered that he was going to hold me and dip me beneath the water, but only for a second, and then he prayed with me.

As he lifted me out of the water seconds later, I experienced absolute peace. Rising out of the pool, I felt my perfect spirit being lifted up and sent soaring throughout the century-old wooden rafters of our church. I hadn't a trace of fear or embarrassment. Then, as I climbed out of the pool wringing wet, my mom waited at the foot of the steps to greet me. She hugged me, my robe wet and clinging to me like a new skin.

I tried fulfilling others' expectations of me in different areas of my life, like when I started to date a girl named Dawn in the ninth grade. Dawn's parents were fundamentalist Christians and wanted to know whether I was saved or not. I told them yes, but they still insisted on praying for me. I thanked them, though I didn't know what for.

That relationship didn't last very long. I was best friends with two other girls who became jealous that I was spending my time with Dawn instead of them, so I broke up with her. One of those friends turned out to be lesbian. As fellow outsiders, we clung to each other even when we didn't understand that our world was against us or why.

As my adolescence got up to full speed, I became increasingly quiet, revealing myself less and less to my family, especially to my mom, a fact that she grilled me on until finally giving up sometime around my mid-to-late-teens. After futile attempts to get into my best friend's pajamas when we spent the night together and only longing glances at and from men in locker rooms at the lake where my family vacationed, I finally had my first sought-after sexual experience at seventeen. It was Senior Skip Day in high school, and my friends and I had skipped out to have lunch at Pizza Hut.

I had discovered, after getting my driver's license, that I enjoyed flirting with truck drivers on the highway, mostly the ultramasculine type: big, bearded, and seemingly hairy everywhere. Maybe I got the truck driver thing from my mom's brother. He wasn't exactly hot; in fact, he was more your typical short and overweight image of truck drivers. But he and his ultimate manual labor fascinated me. I envied his ability to hit the road and escape the mundane responsibilities of providing for a wife and four kids in a trailer. He even offered to take me cross-country with him, an interesting fantasy now, but one I never acted upon.

I would try to make eye contact with the truckers on the highway, without driving into them or off the road, then rub my crotch and see what kind of reaction I got. Most didn't even pay attention; some would realize and flip me off; a few would realize and play along. Pizza Hut guy played along.

He followed me off the highway and into town. I wasn't prepared for whatever he was up to. I thought I'd lost him after a few traffic lights as

I quickly ducked into the Pizza Hut parking lot. Luckily, none of my friends were there yet. But, to my horror and simultaneous excitement, my truck driver pulled around the back of the restaurant and parked directly behind me. I sat frozen in my seat as he climbed out and approached my parent's wood-paneled station wagon. "Is he going to kill me or jump me?" I wondered.

"Hey," was all he said when he got to my half-rolled-down window.

"Hey," I returned.

Then he said something like, "Nice day for a drive," but I don't remember what, if anything, I said in response. Instead, I started playing with myself again through my jeans. He gave the now-standard "Whatcha got goin' there?" and reached one hairy paw inside my window to help. The entire restaurant could have been watching this guy put his hand on my crotch for all I knew or cared. I came the instant he touched me, charged by not only seventeen-year-old hormones but also the thrill of the entire scene.

He wasn't done. He suggested we go inside to really check out each other. "Plus," he said, nodding toward my obvious crotch, "you may have to clean up a bit."

"I guess you're right," I mumbled, my head still spinning. I was waiting for my classmates to round the corner in their own cars any minute, shouting my name. But I safely made it inside the restaurant; he went in one door, I in the other. I discovered I could, and should, move stealthily at times like this. We met in the men's room and he locked the door. Unzipping my pants, he immediately took me in his mouth; I was rock hard again in seconds. He worked his magic for awhile, then I learned to reciprocate for the first time. I bent in front of him and opened my mouth. "I guess this is what you do," I thought. I liked it, and he appeared to like it, so I succeeded in giving my first blow job.

The whole affair didn't take long, but it cemented itself in my memory. As I emerged from the bathroom tucked in and tidy, I saw half of my group already seated around a table in the middle of the restaurant with pitchers of beer. This was before anyone really cared much about carding minors, especially in little redneck towns. "What's up?" my friend Steve asked me when I approached the table. I laughed out loud at the ridiculous situation I was in.

"I need a beer—that's what's up."

I wasn't ashamed of my encounter in the bathroom, though similar experiences later in life left me feeling guilty. I thought for sure that, although my actions felt natural, uncontrolled, motivated by circumstances beyond conscious reasoning, their clandestine nature surely meant that something wasn't altogether right. I soon found the damning passages in the Bible about men lying with other men that seemed to point to my demise. That took another ten years or so to settle.

That day at Pizza Hut, however, I was charged by having pulled off something I thought was outrageous without getting caught. I hadn't gotten caught on the highway, except by someone whom I wanted to catch me; I hadn't gotten caught by my friends; I hadn't gotten caught by the restaurant management or patrons; and, to top it all off, I had eluded further advances from my new friend.

Before he left the bathroom, my truck driver suggested going for a "picnic"—it was such a nice day and all. I wasn't about to push my luck and begged off, but the experience set a number of fantasies into motion. I didn't discover gay bars until I graduated from college and moved out on my own but instead sought out men in parks, rest stops, and the like. I found there were masculine men in those places seeking each other's company, but I was not always quite sure how to find it. Some of the men required a little talk-up; others just wanted silence. Sometimes a hard, anxious dick says more than any mouth can.

I had a number of crushes on friends and classmates in college, though I never dated any of them. I guess I didn't even realize why they called it a "crush" until then; no girl I ever dated left me feeling breathless and happily nervous in her company, or crazed with jealousy if she was with somebody else. One of these crushes during the last semester of my senior year became more serious, as I zeroed in on a loner type named Paul. Paul was officially a sophomore, having returned to college after a stint in the Army with nothing but some government money, a black Mustang convertible, and killer looks. He was the epitome of tall-dark-and-handsome: he was roughly six-three, muscular but lean, with jet black hair and mustache, and a smooth, easy voice.

Once, we bought a keg for a party at my fraternity, put it in the backseat of the Mustang, with the top down, and tooled around town in the snow shouting and turning heads. I was in the front seat next to Paul and on top of the world. My friend Bill was squeezed in back next to the keg, oblivious to the real reason behind my delight.

I was amazed at my own good fortune. Here was a gorgeous guy, four years older than me, world-wise with real money, a real apartment, a real car, and at school simply because he wanted to be, who spent his free time with me. Surely he could have hung out with more sophisticated people. To help maintain his company, I even tried to get him to rush our fraternity. I wanted to be his "big brother," but he eventually figured out that his fraternity days were over.

Nevertheless, we saw each other almost every day. A few times he even spent the night at my fraternity, usually after a party. Once, I woke up to a phone call from Bill, whose room was just down the hall from mine. We went through our usual morning recap and then he said, "Paul's here. Want to talk to him?"

"Paul's where?" I asked, stunned.

"Well, right now he's in my bathroom taking a piss. He spent the night on my couch."

I was dumbfounded. "I'm coming down," was all I said and slammed down the phone. Though at the top of my mind I knew nothing had occurred, I was instantly insane. Throwing open the door to Bill's room, I found them both on the couch watching TV and drinking coffee. "Morning," Paul said, smiling contentedly.

I was speechless for a moment and quickly surveyed the scene: Paul had one leg propped up on the couch. He was wearing jeans with just a white tank top over his chest. His shirt was slung across a chair. Just then, Bill's girlfriend emerged from the back of the room, and I realized my fears were completely unfounded. Feeling suddenly stupid and hoping I hadn't given myself away, I shrank back into my personal hideaway and collapsed on the floor.

That spring, I got a job at the same popular college bar where Paul worked part-time. He was the doorman, checking guys' IDs and letting underage girls slip by, and I was a barback. We didn't always work together, but being in his proximity was enough. At closing time, I'd hang out with Paul, the manager, and the owners of the bar, finally feeling like I was "in the club."

Within these four walls, ceiling, and floors sticky with dried beer was this society of men, an imaginary clubhouse dedicated to male camaraderie, of which the other members of the club were unaware. But when the manager invited Paul and me over to his house to drink beer and watch TV all night, I was keenly aware of its power. I would stay up all night if it meant spending more time with men, just me and the boys. I would gladly risk my schoolwork and endure countless playful taunts for being the youngest member of the club. This was better than any real fraternity.

One night Paul and I were both off work. We stopped at his apartment so he could change clothes for a party we were going to. His place was small and undecorated, consisting mostly of a miniature kitchen and a large, man-sized bed, where I sat while he pulled off his shirt. I tried not to stare, but I could feel my face flush, and I wrung my hands, not knowing where to put them. They felt heavy and in the way, and I was scared that at any moment they would either grab my own crotch or his and shatter my fragile dream. I attempted some trivial conversation.

He crossed the floor in front of me bare-chested and hairy, holding a new shirt. Instead of putting it on, he knelt at an Army footlocker and opened it. I was transfixed by the muscles wrapped around his back like so many pairs of arms. I was sure I didn't have muscles like that. Even his spine was perfect. It was straight as an arrow and dove into his pants and inside his butt. Oh, his butt.

Standing up he held some papers in his hand. He gave them to me and said, "Here, I want you to read something."

Paul knew I was a writer. I had an opinion column in the student newspaper that he read faithfully. What he showed me was his own poetry. It was detailed and difficult to read—heavy, wordy, and rich. I don't remember the specifics of the poems; their complexity is what stays in my mind. They described another outsider: an alien anxious to see life outside of Tennessee, an alien who never really fit the regimen of the U.S. Army, an alien who was too old now for college, commuting to classes with students still wearing their high school letter jackets and class rings.

I couldn't stop myself from crying, but I kept my head bowed, pretending to read. Some of my tears dropped onto the paper and smeared the ink, but I didn't care. I wanted to leave at least some kind of message to him about the turmoil going on inside of me. I knew this was an extremely private thing he was sharing with me, and he must have a reason. See? I understood, Paul!

I pulled myself together enough to wipe my face and look up. Paul was in the bathroom. "These are incredible," I said, almost whispering.

He came out wearing nothing but a pair of gauzy Army green boxer shorts. Instead of looking at me he grabbed a pair of khakis, casually stepped into them, and said, "Thanks. I've had them a long time. I just don't know what to do with them."

"You should publish them!" I exclaimed. "Let the world see them."

He finally looked my way, smiled big, and said, "I don't know. Maybe. They're kind of personal." I held his stare until he reached out his hand for the poems. "Come on. Let's get out of here. We've got trouble to get into tonight. Bill's gonna put out an APB on us pretty soon." I handed them over without saying anything more.

I wanted to believe Paul cared for me in the same way that I cared for him, but I was afraid to risk revealing myself. I wanted *him* to move; I wanted him to toss the papers aside and grab the nape of my neck with his strong, meaty hand and pull my mouth up to his dark, parted lips. I wanted to feel what it felt like to have two mustaches rubbing against each other. I wanted to wrap my arms securely around his back along the same smooth lines as his muscles. I wanted to follow his spine's lead and dive into the back of his pants.

None of this was to happen though. He finished dressing and we left for our party. In fact, little more came of our relationship. We still continued to hang out with each other at work, but Paul quit coming around the fraternity as often as he had that winter. I was never aware of any female competition when I was around Paul, but he clearly wasn't interested in me the way I was interested in him. As my graduation neared, I quit the bar and enjoyed my last few weeks of carefree college life. Over the summer I called Paul at his sister's house in Nashville, but he was never there and finally I gave up.

What I missed most about Paul was his companionship and acceptance. Even though I campaigned to be his fraternal big brother, he had become my big brother in life, showing me things my real brother, my dad, or anyone else never showed me. Paul, unexpectedly for both of us, taught me how to be quiet but confident, masculine but not overtly aggressive. He taught me how to smoke cigarettes correctly, how to take the smoke down my throat without gagging on it or releasing it prematurely, then enjoying the first tingles of nicotine. To this day, fueled by plenty of erotic images from boyhood, thanks to well-placed Marlboro ads in the Sunday *Parade,* I equate smoking with tough masculinity despite, maybe even because of, its deadly effects.

Likewise, though no thanks to Paul, unfortunately, somewhere along the way I also learned to equate masculinity with having lots of sex—spreading your seed whether you were reproducing or just spilling it on some other horny guy's chest. I imagine this to be a holdover from the 1970s, when it was every gay man's "duty" to go forth and fuck, partnered or not. AIDS created a battleground for that notion, one that, I admit, pisses me off for having cheated me out of the real fun, or so I'm told. I had already heard of AIDS when I became sexually active; otherwise, I doubt I would be around today.

Discovering gay bars and, more important, *leather* bars, and all their dangling carrots, when I was twenty-one seemed to be heaven on earth for many years. I found men who were as attractive and stimulating as Paul but could also give me the physical affirmation I had longed for since my uncle told me I didn't belong. Finding the address of the only leather bar in Washington, DC, wasn't difficult; finding the actual building was. It was in a truly shitty part of town, as I would soon discover was the case with many gay bars. One-way streets stopped without warning and changed directions: once flowing merrily with the Sunday afternoon traffic, I was suddenly besieged by cars headed right for me.

It was a typical steamy summer afternoon in DC, and I was more than ready for a cold beer when I finally found the place. I put my thirst on hold for a minute when I opened the door: the place was pitch-black at 6:00 p.m., and the smoke was so thick that the lighted neon beer signs were barely visible. After a few moments I could discern dark figures moving in front of me—men clad in black leather from head to toe or wearing old jeans with a button or two undone, worn workboots, and no shirt. I was thrilled. My God, I could finally reach out and run my fingers through the hair on a man's chest without getting punched.

Instead, I got fucked. After the added courage of two or three beers I got to talking with a guy who was probably forty at the time. That's about the only distinguishing feature I can recall of him now, except that I followed him home that night, not knowing, or caring, what I had gotten myself into. We made out on the floor in front of his fireplace, fulfilling my desire to press my mustache against another man's. What seems so simplistic now made me instantly hard, as we explored each other's mouths with our tongues. Then, he turned me on my stomach, took his time greasing up my ass with his fingers, and slowly mounted me as he held the sides of my hips firmly.

I had been fucked a couple of times before by a man who happened to live next to my fraternity house, but this time it seemed official. He took such care and deliberation in the act. Though I still felt the pain at the outset, my eyes soon rolled back in my head as we both got into sync. I remember spreading my arms out wide on the floor in front of me, trying to grasp something secure. The cool brick in front of the fireplace where my head rested helped ground me in reality and kept me from floating away as he rode.

He came inside of me, and though he was wearing a rubber, I feared that something might have gone wrong, that the rubber might have torn or come off. You don't think this way before your own climax, only after you're on your way back down to earth. Nothing was wrong with the rubber, but the danger would always be a sobering klaxon in my head. That took some of the fun out of my sexual exploits, but it didn't dampen them altogether.

Ironically, it was my parent's early guidance that was most useful to me during these times, though I didn't realize that until much later. Many of the men I met came from homes torn apart by divorce, addictions, or other forms of abuse, and they simply passed on that abuse to their partners.

I think you have to lose a little innocence to appreciate what's left. Though my parents hadn't a clue about my sexuality, or at least we never discussed it, I am indebted to the loving, stable environment in which they raised me. My baptism remains the moment in my life when I experienced the greatest clarity and peace of mind I have ever felt, and I don't deny God's complete, perfect presence there.

I found out that I *did* belong somewhere after all. Though many of my future relationships with men would turn out to be less than stellar, I knew that many others like me were taking the same trip, making the same mistakes, and struggling to forge some kind of normalcy—although I don't think there's ever been a more incomplete word in their daily lives.

−3−

Pump Jockey

Andrew W. M. Beierle

Tony Alexamenos was wet and naked when the pale yellow Cadillac floated into the station, as cool and smooth as a Creamsicle on wheels.

Damn! Who the hell wants gas at seven-thirty on a Saturday morning?

In the darkness of the service station bay, he turned off the hose he had been using to sluice the saltwater from his body, threw his dripping jams on the back of a battered red folding chair, and stepped clumsily into his oil-stained work suit, hopping from one foot to the other as if standing on hot coals. His clean undershorts, glowing like ivory neon in the darkness, lay out of reach on the workbench across the room, where he had left them on his way to the beach.

Outside, the driver laid on the horn.

"Hang on. I'm comin'." *Shit! If the old man wakes up, there'll be no surfing for a week.* He shrugged his arms into the suit and slipped into his flip-flops, shuffling across the gritty concrete until his toes locked into place around the yellow rubber thongs. Crescents of dampness materialized around his armpits and crotch.

The horn sounded again.

"Keep your pants on," Tony muttered, struggling with his own. The overalls' zipper had snagged about two inches below his navel, and he couldn't get it unjammed. But with this horn-happy idiot apparently warming up for a John Philip Sousa march, he decided to abandon modesty in favor of speed and ran toward the garage bay door.

Tony was pissed. The station wouldn't even open for another half hour, and everyone in South Beach knew it. When he'd been in the water not fifteen minutes earlier, he'd had the opportunity to survey the island for signs of life, and he'd seen not a single light in the kitchens or bathrooms of the flat-roofed, Necco-hued houses along the beach, nor in any of the double-wides scattered like jetsam at the Point. And it was way too early for lost tourists, who at this hour would still be snug in their beds, dreaming of their free Continental breakfasts at the Suncoast Quality Inn.

Still, he figured he was lucky. If the waves hadn't been so piss poor, he'd still be in the surf, and if this bastard and his mobile brass section had rolled in here and roused his father from the loving embrace of Jack Daniels, there'd been hell to pay. It wouldn't have mattered to Demetrios that the damn station wasn't even open. He'd have flown into a rage and taken a swipe or two at Tony, who long ago had learned to duck and dodge his boozy father's infamous flying fists.

Tony grunted as he hefted the garage door. Outside was a '59 DeVille convertible in showroom condition, twin bullet taillights mounted in silver bezels on the biggest tail fins the world had ever seen.

"Fill 'er up. Hi-Test," the driver demanded in a croaking voice as Tony walked briskly around the car, his fingers thrumming lightly across the sculpted hood of the idling Caddy. Tony didn't make eye contact, just turned and kept on walking to the stern of the land yacht.

"Yes, sir," Tony said, then added, loud and flat, "Engine off." He was damned if he was going to kiss butt before he was even on the clock. He busied himself at the ancient pump, its red paint scabrous with rust.

The man in the car wore a Panama hat a couple sizes too big and an oversized pair of sunglasses that effectively masked the upper half of his face. He was huge, a blimp, and it appeared that all he was wearing was a bathrobe. Tony didn't want to know if there was anything under it. Definite pervert. That explained the hat and glasses. Probably planned on distributing candy to minors.

Sliding his sunglasses down his sunburned nose, the driver peered into the rearview mirror directly at Tony's reflected image. Sensing that he was being watched, Tony turned his head. Their eyes met on the silvered surface, but the driver instantly looked away, mumbling something indecipherable.

"Sir?" Tony said, anticipating a rebuke. People always did that. They want to complain but don't have the balls to actually say anything, so they mutter into their armpits or elbows for their own sake or the benefit of their passengers.

"Yes?" the man said, returning his sunglasses to the bridge of his nose with his right index finger but not looking back at Tony.

"You said something, sir?"

"No no no, my dear boy. Just thinking out loud."

My dear boy. Must be British or something. Yeah, right, *British.* The damn pump pressure was low again, and filling the tank on this boat would take an eternity. It gave Tony the opportunity to carefully inspect the car. For ten years old, this one was absolutely cherry—not a single ding or dent, not a trace of the salty residue that blanketed cars every night and ate away at them all day. The white convertible boot was brilliant and supple, free from the green-black mildew that, in the primordial mists of central Florida, attacked anything remotely hospitable. Even the spikes in the car's decorative rear grille looked as if they had been recently flossed.

The interior was a different story. The rear seat was awash to the armrests in boxes, paper cups, and foil wrappers from every fast food joint in Sugar Mill Beach: Krystal, Kentucky Fried Chicken, Krispy Kreme, even Astro Burger, the mom-and-pop fast food shack out Highway 1 toward Titusville.

"Check your oil, sir?" Tony asked as he screwed on the filler cap.

"By all means!"

By all means, my ass. Tony was familiar with that falsetto of exaggerated enthusiasm. It was the same tone of voice the Big Bad Wolf had used on Little Red Riding Hood. *The better to eat you with, my dear.* Tony knew when he was being hit on; it happened to him all the time. All of them were creeps: the skinny Italian guy from Miami with the see-through shirt and iridescent pants, the fat shoe salesman who offered Tony the pick of any of the footwear in his trunk, the pasty-faced man from New Jersey with a station wagon full of wife and kids who lured him into the men's room on the pretext that the john was overflowing and then got down on his knees and begged Tony— begged him—to let him have at it. It was pitiful. Each and every one of them said he wouldn't have to do anything but "sit back and enjoy it," but he wondered what on God's green earth made them think he would enjoy anything that involved bodily contact with them. When Tony first declined their invitations, they invariably offered him cash, but he was even more disgusted by the way they humiliated themselves. No amount of money would convince Tony to surrender himself to this joker today, should he ask, and he probably would. He'd rather feed his family jewels to a meat grinder.

But, Tony thought, there was still a way to profit from an encounter with this sorry sack o' shit. He could easily scam this dumb fuck by telling him his shocks are shot, which was obvious. He would replace only those on the driver's side but charge him for all four. Tony had learned the art of the scam from his father. Much of the station's income was bilked from hapless tourists who rolled in looking for directions to Turtle Mound or the old sugar mill ruins and rolled out with four brand-new tires or a new transmission and a tale of woe that would make the distinguished gentlemen over at the Better Business Bureau of East Central Florida piss purple for a week.

"Everything looks fine under here, sir," Tony called out, leaning his head around the upraised hood. "But you know, it looks like you could do with some new shocks. Leastwise you ought to let me check 'em out."

"I couldn't possibly today," the man said, "but I will come back for a complete inspection under your skilled and capable hands. Now, how much do I owe you?"

"Seven twenty-five, sir." *And I'll be keeping my skilled and capable hands to myself, Dumbo.*

The man peeled off a ten from a greasy roll of bills. "Here you are . . . Did you ever tell me your name?"

Tony squinted off into the distance while turning the ten spot over in his hands. "It's Tony."

"Well, Tony, you are a very fine young man who provides excellent service. I'm sorry I was so impatient when I pulled in. Take this for your trouble." He pressed a second greasy bill into Tony's hand.

"Thing is, we ain't even open yet."

"I understand."

The driver started the car, put it in gear, and fishtailed onto the highway in a cloud of sand, gravel, and broken shells. Tony looked at the bill the man had crushed into his hand. A fifty. "Shit yes!" he said. This was, without a doubt, the biggest tip he had ever received, if indeed it was a tip and not a mistake. Probably thought the fifty was a five.

Tony went into the station's office, which, even though two of its walls were floor-to-ceiling glass, always managed to look cramped, dark, and dingy. The eight-by-ten room was cluttered with oil cans and spare parts, and on a ledge along the front window, peppered with dead houseflies, were faded copies of *Popular Science, Field and Stream, True,* and *Reader's Digest* magazines that customers had left behind. He banged open the ancient black cash register, made change for the ten, which he pocketed with his fifty—*his* fifty—and, whistling, went out back to hose off his surfboard before the predictable lineup of South Beach sad sacks arrived, wanting a buck's worth of gas and some free air for their nearly bald blackwalls.

Tony never understood how his father put food on the table and clothes on their backs with the income the station generated, though, come to think of it, food got to be spotty at times and Tony bought most of his clothes himself with his earnings from his other jobs— lifeguarding and working at the surf shop. As he saw it, the main problem with the station was location. It sat at the dead end of a dead-end road on a dead-end island, with the wide blue Atlantic on one side and Mosquito fucking Lagoon on the other.

Thank God for the students from the college. Every September, when the streets of Sugar Mill Beach filled with bright, shiny new sports cars bearing license plates from Virginia, New York, and Massachusetts, business picked up at South Beach Gulf. Instead of ten-year-old Chevy Bel Air station wagons eaten away by rust, Tony serviced muscle cars: 'Vettes, Goats, and Chevy Malibu SS convertibles, with the occasional racing green TR-6 thrown in. The cars belonged to students at Sanctuary College, the elite Sugar Mill Beach school that was a lesser-known academic rival of such respected Magnolia League schools as Duke, Emory, and Vanderbilt.

A surprising number of the sports cars ended up at South Beach Gulf for repairs, considering the ten-mile drive to an area that, other than being home to Gator Grove, the second largest mobile home park in the state of Florida, had no points of interest whatsoever. But on the Sanctuary campus, Demetrios Alexamenos had a reputation for cheap, reliable service—cheap mostly because Tony did the work at something less than minimum wage, and reliable because he *never* ripped off Sanctuary students, who were worth a good four years of repeat business and invaluable word of mouth.

Demetrios did not allow the students in the bays while he worked, but if he was out cold, which was more and more the case lately, Tony didn't mind if they stood in the doorway or even came in and talked to him, as long as they didn't touch anything and then complain about getting grease on the starched and monogrammed Oxford broadcloth shirts they wore with oversized khaki or Madras shorts and those damn penny loafers without socks. It was less aggravating to divert them with small talk than to have them whine every fifteen minutes about how long it was taking or repeat that they had better things to do than "hang around this filthy grease pit." He despised them for their money, their privilege, and their snot-nosed attitudes but tolerated them because he loved working on their cars. When they weren't around, he could take joyrides in roadsters he would otherwise never have the opportunity to sit in, let alone drive.

Tony generally could discern which of the customers were straight arrows and which were a little bent. The straight boys talked about nothing but themselves, their cars, their fraternities, and their girlfriends, typically in that order. But the others were interested only in Tony. How old was he? Did he go to school? Was that his surfboard? Ever get into town? Can I have your phone number? Tony pointed out that the telephone number was on the receipt, but none of them ever called, other than to complain about something. Maybe they were just making up the problem to talk to Tony and were waiting for him to ask them to bring the car back. But Tony was sure of his work and busy enough that he didn't need to waste time checking out, for free, a nonexistent problem for some Sanctuary stud with a hard-on for him. It might be different if he thought something would really happen, but Tony knew all of them would scream rape if he laid one greasy hand on their pretty pastel Polo shirts.

A week later, Tony was sitting in the gas station office waiting for his best buddy, Charlie Pickering—Pick to his friends. Tony and Pick were going to throw their boards in the back of Pick's '52 Chevy pickup and drive down to Sebastian Inlet.

Tony sat with one clunky work boot, loosely laced, on the floor, the other atop the gray metal desk. He was leaning back in the green-vinyl-covered chair, snapping his gum and tossing loose screws and washers into the trash barrel across the room. He got out of the chair when he heard the Chevy hacking and grinding to a halt. Pick, a gangly redhead whose body was dappled with a network of freckles the color of Georgia clay, bounded out of the cab and slammed the door. His face was alight with excitement.

"Tony, I know who your mystery man is!" He was out of breath. "You know—the oinker in the yellow caddy."

"Shhhhh! The old man don't need to hear this." Tony was expecting his father to relieve him any minute now. "So who is it?"

"Dallas Eden. Dallas fucking Eden!" Dallas Eden was well known in Sugar Mill Beach, and Edensgate, the home he shared with his mother, silent film star Eve Eden, was a showplace more worthy of Palm Beach or Newport than the tiny coastal town north of Cape Canaveral where it was secluded at the edge of the Sanctuary College campus.

"You're shittin' me. Dallas *Eden?*"

"One and the same. I'm surprised you didn't recognize him."

"Me too, but I couldn't hardly see his face with those sunglasses and that hat. Plus, I didn't think he had gotten that fat. Christ, the guy was disgusting. So how do you know it's him?"

"My cousin Jimmy told me. He works at the ABC Liquor on Tropicana, and some guy's been pullin' up to the drive-through for a couple of weeks in that same yellow Caddy and picking up a couple of fifths of Jim Beam and some paper cups. Anyway, he's got one of them American Express cards, and sometimes he uses it if he don't have cash on him, so Jimmy's seen his name. Figures he drives around looking for nice, juicy teenage boys, gets 'em drunk, and . . . you know, bingo-bango!" Pick snapped his fingers like a lounge singer. "Jimmy says he gives 'em money so they don't squeal to the cops. And Tony boy, it looks like your number has come up! Why else would he give you a fifty-buck tip?"

"Christ, Pick, you make it sound like it's good news. Like I've won the Irish Sweepstakes or something."

"Tony, it *is* good news! Jimmy says if the creep *really* likes you *and* you play hard to get, you could walk away with some major payola. Some guys he wants bad enough he gives 'em cars!"

"I'm not buying *any* of this shit, Pick. Besides, think of what you're asking me to do. The guy's a fucking creep, for Christ's sake."

"Hey, I'm not asking you to marry the guy. Just let the perv' do his stuff, and you drive away in a candy-apple-red Corvette convertible." Pick tried to cover up his exasperation. He knew Tony didn't like to be pressured.

"If you want the car so bad, *you* do it."

"Tony, *you* don't pick this guy; *he* picks you."

"How can you be so sure I'll get a car? And who's to say after five knob jobs I actually get a 'Vette? This ain't the fuckin' *Price Is Right*. What if he ain't feeling all that generous and gives me a fuckin' Dodge Dart instead? I don't care *how* rich you are; you just don't go around giving away free cars like it's some sort of church raffle."

"He's a *Dunstan*, Tony. They *own* Sugar Mill Beach and everyone in it. And he's gonna get *everything* when his old lady kicks. Jimmy said he read in the *Babbler* where she's got one foot on a banana peel and the other on a roller skate right now."

"Yeah, well I wouldn't believe any of the garbage they print in that rag."

"Okay, go ahead and piss on the damn Corvette. But the next time your fuckin' van breaks down—if you ever even get it running again— don't call *me* to come to the rescue. You're makin' a big mistake, Tony, my friend. You have *no* idea what this could mean for you."

Tony knew—knew pretty specifically—what this could mean. He knew what Dallas Eden was looking for, and he shriveled at the thought of it. And he knew a damn sight better than Charlie Pickering what it meant to get a blow job from another guy. Or to give one. For nearly three years he had had what he called "an outhouse romance" with Mitch Novak, their old Gulf delivery man, right there in the men's room at the station. Tony had idolized Mitch since the day he first laid eyes on him, when he was just ten. Mitch was from over Ocala way— horse country—and stepping down from the cab of his tanker truck, he could have just as well been jumping from the driver's seat of a stage coach at some Arizona way station. He wore black stovepipe jeans, a chambray work shirt with the sleeves hacked off at the arm holes, and a dirty, sweat-stained cowboy hat. Coiled around his right forearm, stretching from elbow to hand, was a faded rattlesnake tattoo, ending with its mouth split between his thumb and index finger so he could make it open and shut like it was going to bite. It scared the piss out of Tony when he was younger, but in later years he worshiped it.

Once when Mitch put him in a headlock, Tony caught a whiff of his armpit; mostly it smelled of Dial soap and Old Spice deodorant, but there was enough sweat in it to give it a sharp, sour bite Tony never forgot. It was like a pinch in his pants. Nothing *really* happened until three years ago, when he turned fifteen. He'd seen it coming, like an eighteen-wheeler overtaking him on a steep decline, horn blowing, lights flashing, until he just put it in neutral and let the damn thing roll over him.

Tony had been drawn to men since long before he had words for his feelings, before he knew his desires were different, forbidden. As a child, he directed his affections toward his favorite male TV stars. He lived for each weekly episode of *77 Sunset Strip, Surfside Six,* and *Hawaiian Eye,* all detective shows in exotic locales, with plenty of opportunities for the leading men to wear bathing suits. In particular, he had crushes on Edd Byrnes and Robert Conrad. He frequently invented situations in which his two friends were shirtless—sometimes in just their BVDs—bound and gagged by villains and desperate for his assistance. He toyed with them, savoring the sight of them sweating, struggling against their bonds, until it became clear that the bad guys were coming back from buying cigarettes and the three of them had better vamoose on the double. When he got a little older, his heart throbbed all the more appreciatively for Bob Conrad as James West, who was, conveniently, stripped to the waist and suspended above quicksand and alligator pits by cheesy Mexican banditos with some regularity.

As near as he could recollect, it was in the eighth grade, when other boys began to notice that girls bulged beneath their sweaters, that he genuinely appreciated how guys bulged below their belts. He wanted to touch and smell other boys, and yet he knew, knew *absolutely,* that he couldn't. But try as he might, he couldn't keep his eyes off the chino- and corduroy-covered crotches of his classmates, even the thugs and bullies. *Especially* the thugs and bullies.

He was fourteen when he accidentally stumbled across a mention of "homosexuality" in an Ann Landers book for teenage girls he'd found in the backseat of a car he was servicing. The book wasn't terribly specific about the consequences of *being* a homosexual, but it didn't make it sound like the adventure of a lifetime. From then on, Tony read everything he could find about the subject in the Sugar Mill Beach Library, which was precious little. A couple of years later, on parts runs to Jacksonville, he made time to search the stacks at that city's public library. What information he could find often came in obscure, dusty books bound in what looked like reptile skin. They were of little help—too dry, too technical. He wasn't interested in charts and graphs of "galvanic skin response," whatever the hell that was. He wanted somebody to tell him what to do with these feelings. None of the authorities gave any indication how widespread a phenomenon it was, and certainly none of them encouraged it. The thought that there might be significant numbers of homosexuals in the world, perhaps even in the state of Florida, did not occur to him at first, nor could he imagine how he would identify such a person.

Tony had dated girls since the ninth grade, with little emotion and no real consequence. Girls were so attentive to him that he felt he had no choice. He'd take them to Daytona Beach, where they'd walk on the boardwalk hand in hand, eat pizza and Italian ice, play a few games of Skiball, and ultimately head for the band shell or a deserted stretch of beach, more at her urging than his. He necked without benefit of instruction, and he liked the way it felt to kiss and be kissed. But he was never really interested in much else. Sometimes the girl would guide his hand to one of her breasts, and he instinctively knew to gently rub or squeeze it, to appear surprised and appreciative of the opportunity, and to ratchet up the kissing and the moans. But he might as well have been kneading a pound of Play-Doh. The path of passion, so clearly marked for other boys his age, was a dead end to him.

Tony felt differently about boys—they were awesome and beautiful in a way ninth and tenth grade girls were not. He'd go to wrestling matches or track meets to cheer on his favorites, and in the process he developed the image of a regular guy, sports-minded, school-spirited—the farthest possible thing from a pansy or a fag, epithets frequently applied to members of the math club or the AV crew. *If only they knew why I was really here,* he'd think, as he'd watch one wrestler put a scissor lock on the other so the underdog's face was but an inch from his competitor's crotch. And then with a wink, a smile, and the sliding of the flimsy lock on the men's room door, Mitch Novak answered the questions Tony had been asking himself all these years.

Tony kept his every-other-Saturday trysts with Mitch for three years. And, of course, he thought about Mitch on those occasions, twice or three times a day, when he beat off. Then, just three months ago, Tony was awakened from his reveries of Mitch—permanently. On the first Saturday of March, he was waiting in the office for Mitch with his usual preemptive hard-on. He had leaped out of bed at six, half an hour early, and struggled into his jams with an erection that just wouldn't quit. His pop was in Tampa on family business, and for the first time he and Mitch could actually use a bed—get completely naked and *make love* in his bed.

Mitch knew Tony's old man would be gone—he must have told him three times last trip—and he promised to be there as early as possible. But when the dusty Westclox inside the toy tire, a promotion for the Goodyear store in Daytona, struck eight, Mitch was nowhere to be seen. He had never been late, not once. And this time he said he'd be there early, so they'd have more time to themselves.

There could be only one explanation: he'd had an accident. The rig had jackknifed on I-4 and fallen into Lake Monroe. Or worse, Mitch had struck an abutment, the truck had exploded, and he'd been trapped, burned alive, beating against the window with his fist, a boot, a flashlight, anything, until it was too late.

At nearly ten-thirty, paralyzed with fear and anticipating the worst, Tony at last felt the familiar low rumble of the rig coming up through the floor. He jumped up and ran to the door, bracing himself on either side and leaning out for his first glimpse of the blue-and-orange cab and gleaming silver tank. But it wasn't Mitch behind the wheel. It was a small man who didn't fill up the windshield the way Mitch did. Tony flexed his arms against the door frame and pushed himself back into the office. He sat down at the desk and opened an *Argosy* magazine, ring-stained from where his pop had set his cold beers down. He heard the truck's brakes shiver with a pneumatic sneeze and then the door of the cab open and shut. A pair of boots squinched over the gravel, and a weaselly looking fellow stuck his head in the door.

"I got a delivery here for a Demetrios Alex . . . ?" His teeth were as brown as bark—he chawed all right—and he could hold a stogie in his mouth with his jaws shut thanks to the absence of a couple of his upper teeth.

"Alexamenos," Tony said, trying to sound casual, though he was nearly breathless. "You got the right place."

"Awright then." The man spit into his hands, rubbed them together, and disappeared back out the doorway. Once the gas was flowing, Tony got up and peeked out the window for a better look at this varmint. He'd taken off his cap and was scratching his head and smoothing a few strands of dirt-colored hair across his bald spot, which was brown as a nut, except where it was flaking off, leaving patches of pink and white.

Foremost in Tony's mind was Mitch's whereabouts, but he wondered how was he going to find out what happened to him without letting this hayseed know something was afoot. He thought that no matter what he said, his lust and anxiety would immediately be obvious. But hell, Mitch had been the regular driver for nearly eight years. It was only natural for a customer to inquire about him.

Tony got up and walked outside, real casual like, feigning an interest in the broken thermometer hanging on the wall, snapping it twice with his index finger as if it hadn't been broken since dinosaurs ruled the earth. How should he phrase it? Don't ask about Mitch; ask about "the regular driver," as if he didn't know his name. That'll throw him off the scent.

"Say, where's the regular driver?"

"Mitch Novak? Hoo-boy, is his sorry ass in the sling! Let me tell you, I shore wouldn't want to trade places with him today."

Tony felt like someone had stuffed a whole loaf of soft white bread down his throat. "Whatdya mean?" he managed to choke out.

"How old are you, boy?"

"Eighteen," Tony said. "Almost."

The runt had his mouth all screwed up and his right hand was holding up his stubbly chin. "Well, I guess you're old enough to be told the truth, which is that ol' Mitchy was caught with his pants down with the Lamar twins over to Sanford, the two of 'em, Matt and Andy, diddlin' Mitch, when their daddy walked in on 'em. Jasper Lamar was s'posed to be off fishin', but there was a big algae bloom on Lake Monroe and he didn't want to put in the boat. Came back to the station and found the "Out to Lunch" sign in the office window. Guess we know what kind of lunch meat was bein' served."

Tony had been to the Sanford Gulf on 17-92 a couple of times to pick up some parts. Sanford was a sorry-assed place, like South Beach, with nothing to recommend it but some tired zoo down by the lake that looked more like the county dog pound. Tony'd met Matt and Andy Lamar, but they hadn't impressed him as being queer. They were good-looking, like Ricky Nelson or Fabian with blond hair, and they were jocks—Matt lettered in football, Andy in wrestling—but what the hell was Mitch doing messing around with them?

"You mean he's been fired?" His heart sank.

"Fired? Hell, boy, he was damn near kilt!"

"What? How?"

"They say Jasper went berserk. You would too, you see both your young 'uns servin' this pervert's twisted needs. Well, Mitch got himself zipped up lickety split and ran for his truck, but Jasper brought him down with a tire iron to the head. He dragged Mitch back into the men's room and whupped him sumpin' turble. Lost an eye and most all his teeth. Way I heard it, Jasper was about to cut Mitch's balls off when some Seminole County deputies pulled up. Mitch was a bloody pulp lyin' on the men's room floor, and at first the cops thought it was Jasper they was s'posed to arrest! Then Jasper told them Mitch had been havin' carnal relations with the two boys, and that was another thing entirely. They cuffed Mitch quicker'n you can snuff a match. Then they called a ambulance so's not to get their black-and-white red all over. Pretty funny, eh? Black-and-white red all over?"

"Yeah. Ha-ha." Tony didn't know whether to cry, throw up, or force the gas hose down the throat of this foul-mouthed bastard, who was obviously enjoying every delicious bit of gossip about his co-worker. He was scared and sorry Mitch was hurt, but mostly he couldn't bring himself to believe that Mitch would do with other guys the things they did together. He *worshiped* Mitch. What they had was special, not something common and filthy, even though they'd only ever done it in a rest room.

"Now get this: Matt's the one had called the cops—to *stop* the beatin'—and neither one of them snot-nosed young 'uns would stand by what their daddy was sayin' to the police. They said they ain't never done nothin' like their daddy said and didn't know why their paw and Mitch was thrashin' it out. Can you imagine that? Those boys sided with that homo!"

Tony was trembling. He hoped the slimeball wouldn't notice. "So is Mitch going to go to jail?"

"Hell no. Not with both boys sayin' Mitch ain't done nothin'. It's Jasper's word against Mitch's. See, where Jasper went wrong was he went too far. Bunged Mitch up bad, real bad. Anyways, they agreed not to file no sex molestin' charges against Mitch if he agreed not to press charges of assault with intent to kill against the kids' old man. The police said one or two licks to subdue the bastard would have been satisfactory and then call the law in, but Mitch was mighty tore up. Half-blinded, like I said." The peckerwood spit into his right hand and smoothed down his flyaway hair, pulled on his cap, and tugged twice on the greasy brim. "Why're you so interested in Mitch Novak anyways? He didn't slip *you* his sausage, did he?"

Tony could barely control himself. He'd as soon kill this freakish little rodent as look at him.

"It ain't nothing like that. He's just been our Gulf man for about as long as I can remember. He seemed like a nice guy. I never thought nothing like this would happen to him."

"He done brought it on hisself."

"So you're gonna be the regular on this route?"

"Looks that way," he said, lifting himself into the cab.

Tony's shift could not end soon enough, and even though Demetrios was only five minutes late, it seemed like five hours. He had filled the van's gas tank the minute he'd decided to go Sanford and was ready to leave when his pop walked in. "Hey, Pop. Got somethin' to do" was all he said, and he jumped in the van and laid rubber his threadbare tires could ill afford. He took the back roads through the celery fields and made good time, despite the difficulty of passing farm equipment on the two-lane blacktop. It was not quite three when he arrived at Seminole Memorial, his dusty face streaked with sweat and tears.

The hospital's foyer was cool and quiet, the burgundy-and-black floors recently buffed, the faintest of medicinal smells in the air. A sign near the front desk indicated that visiting hours were about to begin and would last until 6 p.m. Behind the desk, a plump woman with powdered cheeks answered the phone while sorting large index cards with colored tabs on their edges. Tony approached her.

"I'd like to see Mitch Novak. Can you tell me where he is?" Tony hoped the quaver in his voice wasn't noticeable.

"Let me check," the nurse said, pleasantly. "Are you family? Mr. Novak's visitors are family only."

"Yes, ma'am, I am," Tony said, then drew a blank. "I'm his uncle . . . I mean, he's my uncle, ma'am."

She looked at him over her bifocals. "Very well then, your uncle is in room two-twenty. Don't stay too long. He hasn't got much stamina."

Tony had bolted for the elevators as soon as she had given him the number. He kept repeating it over and over. Two-twenty. Two-twenty. Two-twenty. He felt like he was going to crap his pants. Outside the room, he took a deep breath and pushed on the door.

Inside, the blinds were drawn and the room was dark. Tony moved toward the bed. Had he not seen Mitch's name in a little plastic slot on the door, Tony would not have been certain it was him. Mitch's nose, which had been broken in two places, was set and braced; his entire upper face and head was in a cast; and his mouth was held slightly open by metal braces. Tony saw only three teeth in the front part of his mouth. His head was immobilized, and his left arm was in a cast. But the most frightening thing was that his head cast only had one eye hole in it.

"Holy shit, Mitch! What the fuck did he do to you?"

The gritty sound of plaster moving against bed sheets was the only indication that Mitch was conscious and had heard him. Unable to turn his head, he motioned with his good arm for the owner of the voice to come closer. When Tony was within reach, Mitch grasped his T-shirt with his good arm and pulled him closer, almost up to his face. After a few seconds, he grunted and pushed him away.

"Mitch. Geez. I freaked out when I heard. Christ, it's every bit as bad as he said it was."

With obvious difficulty, Mitch managed to pushed out a sound, "oo?"

"The guy who replaced you. He looks like a half-dead old rat."

Mitch convulsed and issued another one-syllable word, but Tony couldn't understand it.

"I swear to God, I'll kill the bastard! I will. I'll kill him tonight!"

Mitch waved his hand back and forth as if to say, "No, that won't be necessary, thank you."

"Mitch, I'll stand by you. I'll see you through this, I swear. I *love* you, Mitch."

Tony could not have been more hurt by what happened next. In the same way Mitch had told Tony not to kill Jasper Lamar, he waved his hand back and forth. *Not necessary. Not interested. Don't bother.*

"But, Mitch, I—" His words were swallowed when Mitch grabbed him by the shirt again and pulled him even closer.

"O!" Mitch's mouth smelled rank, like Listerine and shit. He released him with a snap and Tony fell backward. Then he motioned for Tony to give him the pad and pencil on the bedside table. He had trouble writing with one hand until Tony caught on and steadied the pad for him. Mitch released the pad and coughed. The message was sloppy, but Tony was able to make it out. "GET OUT DONT COME BACK."

Mitch made one more grunt-word, which sounded to Tony like either "Out!" or "Now!"

Tony ran from the room, the horrible smell of Mitch's breath clinging to his own nose and lips, still feeling the deathly grasp of Mitch's clawlike hand reaching through his T-shirt to crush his heart. Outside the hospital, he was overcome by the sensation, at once familiar and confusing, that he was back in a world in which no one loved him—and no one ever would.

Happy Birthday

Daniel M. Jaffe

My Darling Boy,

Happy Birthday!
Don't tell me you're surprised; you knew I'd write. I am your mother, after all. I apologize for not actually being able to bring myself to write this letter, but you understand. That's why you're writing the letter for me. I know.

Everything is fine here in old Texarkana (the Texas side of the border, if you please, not that immoral Arkansas-Clinton side!), just as you left it. Dad's in the garden yanking on those weeds that sprout up every June, that infiltrate and threaten his flower bed. Never have I seen a man go on so about petunias like your father. Nothing but petunias. Yellow ones, white ones, purple ones, but no pinks. He thinks I've forgotten it was you who first brought home petunias for your seventh grade science project. I couldn't abide that project, testing whether chemical or natural fertilizers would be more effective on petunias. Where on earth did you get such an idea? And where did you ever find the natural fertilizer? Never mind, I don't want to know. I never did want to know.

Ever since seventh grade, Dad's been out there every spring. More after you went away to college. Even more after that day, that awful day, when you told us your news.

Dad gives those petunias all his attention. No substitute for you, of course.

Sometimes I think back to that dreadful day, that day when you told us about . . . about your . . . situation.

I realize now you didn't mean to hurt us by divulging those horrid privacies. (You couldn't have known what would cause a parent pain; you'll never know that, will you?) You just couldn't have meant to hurt us as badly as you actually did. You were always a caring son; it wasn't in you to inflict such pain on your parents, not intentionally. If I thought, for one minute, for one solitary second, that you'd intended so ruthlessly to devastate us like you did, why I'd . . . I'd . . . I don't know—I'd . . . never quilt another blanket cover, never stir another pot of grits. How I hate remembering that dreadful day!

The morning started out so normally. "Henry," I said to Dad, "this is a wonderful spring day. A normal, wholesome, God-given spring day, and I love it. Thank you, Lord." Son, you know I said just that because I always say just that on normal spring mornings. My own little prayer to thank the Lord for the day. I know I should thank Him when it rains, too, but somehow I just can't bring myself to. (Don't want to encourage Him in that, I guess.)

Dad packed my pink suitcase in the trunk and his blue one beside it.

I didn't pack your goodies in the trunk with the suitcases that day. Oh no. In front, on my lap, I held my big black purse filled with chocolate chip cookies I'd baked for you, baked with butter, not with the margarine I use for us now that your Dad's way too paunchy for his own good. And on top of the big black purse, I piled two cardboard boxes I wheedled out of old Mrs. Morgan at the bakery—"They're for my boy, Mrs. Morgan, my boy"—each box filled with a pecan pie I'd made from scratch from pecans I'd picked from our tree out front—Remember that tree you used to climb like a squirrel?—pecans that I shelled with my own fingers, cracking my nails, shelling them for you. Two pies on my lap and I was uncomfortable, let me tell you, but they were for you.

Dad whined that I shouldn't be bringing you so much food—"We pay good money for his board over there"—but if I didn't bring you your goodies, you'd think that Mom had stopped loving you. I know how you think.

That was how that day began. To cheer myself up when my mind drifts back, I pretend you're here.

I baked your favorite cake today, not that you'll be able to snake your tongue halfway across the country to taste it. But just imagine stepping onto the front porch, hearing that middle plank creak (your father still hasn't fixed that plank), shoving the door open with your shoulder (yes, it still swells and sticks during the humidities), feeling the warm breeze from the kitchen fan at the end of the hallway, that breeze carrying the "parade of aroma floats," as you would say. Just imagine walking into the house that way, into the kitchen, the way you used to after swim practice, all ravenous and drippy-haired, whipping your head back and forth to spray me like a wet, shaggy dog, just to chase me out of the kitchen so you could poke around and follow your nose and see what goodies I'd baked. Well, no need to guess about today. It was a birthday cake, of course. A chocolate, chocolate chip cake with coffee icing. Your favorite. What else on your birthday?

Just picture yourself sniffing at it, dabbing at it with your pinky, smoothing a knife over the indent mark your little finger had made, thinking I wouldn't notice that the icing had been messed with, that something about my cake was not quite right, that somehow my creation had been marred, was not as I had intended it, designed it, planned it, made it with my very own hands, parts of my very own body.

The kitchen's still warm from the fifty minutes at 350 degrees. Feel the warmth. See me sitting by the table in the red apron that I made, every stitch in place, each thread tied tight, the sweetheart neckline perfect to accentuate my high cheekbones, the skirt long enough to protect all my clothing, the pink tulips embroidered on the upper right corner in just the position I had intended. Almost everything I create turns out precisely the way I want it to. Almost.

I'm sitting there out of reach of the electric kitchen fan, waving before my face the Chinese fake-silk hand fan you gave me for my birthday when you were just seven. Remember? You saw it in Chicago's Chinatown when Dad took you on that special vacation to the Windy City, just his "big man" little ten-year-old boy and him. And you saw that fan and told him that's what you wanted to get me for my birthday. And Dad looked at you with that wrinkle-eyed look he gives whenever he wants to show you he thinks you're a bit foolish but wants to respect your right to be so, when he won't say anything, but will just look at you and wonder. Remember that look? Remember that fan?

Remember how you used to hold onto Dad's hand when you'd cross the street and not budge until he said it was okay, how you would cross as soon as he said it was okay? He once tested you, do you remember? Traffic was coming fast and furious, but he told you it was okay to go, so you started to, and he had to yank you back. Remember? He pulled you back and saved you because he loved you. Loves you. Loved you. He saved you. You held onto his hand so he could save you. You let him save you, then. My Abraham and his little Isaac.

How's your job, son? Do you still like acting? Are you finding work? Are you fed?

What kind of acting do you do? I wonder always. Speaking parts? Do you still play all those characters like you did in high school? A romantic lead, maybe? If so, I'm glad I can't see it. That would be a cruelty, watching you onstage kissing a girl, knowing it all to be a hideous lie.

Are you on Broadway, with your name in lights like we always used to pretend when you were in those high school plays? Are you famous yet, son? A Broadway star? Send me your autograph.

We never thought you'd wander so far from home. Not for good. Are you still in New York, even? It's a big city, son. It can be scary, really scary. Never thought you'd not be here on your birthday. Remember Dad tugging your little hand and saving you?

We're right here if you need us, right where you left us, just a hop, skip, and a jump off Route 30. Just follow the big yellow-and-red KOA signs for Campgrounds of America, zip past those chugging trailers and RVs and such, and you'll find us. In a regular house. A stable home right in the heart of America. Smack in the middle of Tornado Alley where a good Christian life can be uprooted and tossed to high heaven in the blink of an eye. And ripped to shreds. You know.

It's a shame you took your diploma with you. We'd have been so proud to hang it in your room. Although Dad might have smashed it. But if it had survived, it would have hung nicely over the head of your blue-quilted bed in the corner. I made that quilt.

I miss nighttimes the most. Oh, I know it's been a good twenty years since I tucked you into bed at night. But I still miss those times.

I bet you don't remember what you would make me do each night before you'd go to sleep. Do you remember? You used to be so afraid of the goblins and demons that you wouldn't let me turn out the light until I checked under your bed and in the closet and sang—well, maybe "sang" is the wrong word—until I chanted, "Demons, devils go away! Goblins, witches, we won't play! We don't like you, never will! If you come, we'll make you ill!" Then I'd swirl around, waving my arms and snapping my fingers like a banshee, and I'd tell you about sweet fairies enchanting the bayous of the Mississippi Delta and you'd fall asleep. . . . A mistake, telling you about the fairies.

Sometimes in the morning as I sit at the makeup vanity table and unroll my curlers, I look into the mirror and wonder what it was you used to see when you looked at me. Couldn't have been the me I see. I didn't think it so terrible to let you see me in my hair net or in cold cream or with the mud pack. Did I frighten you? Did I make you think all women look so ugly at their vanities? When I wonder about these things my stomach clutches and makes those gurgling noises you used to claim were impolite at the dinner table: "Mom, teach your insides manners!" you would say and smirk, all proud that you'd caught me being rude at the table. When I hear those gurgles of mine, I wonder whether maybe it was my insides that repulsed you. That makes more sense in a way. I swallow bicarb every day, but I just can't stop my stomach gurgles.

How's your life, son? How's your life, so far away? Where are you? No more letters. Are you at that same return address? I do want to know, really do. We both do. Sorry about those phone calls. Don't know what came over me, why I refused to accept the charges. I wasn't used to such calls, I suppose, never had been asked to accept a collect call before. And then when you called direct afterward, I suppose I . . . I suppose I . . . just didn't recognize your voice or something— that's all—that's why I hung up. It really wasn't because it was you calling, sweetheart. It wasn't you. In fact, it wasn't even you calling, actually, was it? Not my baby, the boy I'd raised.

And you know I'm not one for correspondence, so how could you expect me to answer your letters? And how could you expect me to write you a Happy Birthday letter when you know I hate to write? And when I'm not even sure of your return address? So you can't expect me to write this letter to you. I'm glad you're doing it for me.

I love you, son. You didn't believe what I said, did you? About not loving you anymore? What mother on earth could stop loving her boy? Would stop loving him just because of something he said? Not me. I'm not that petty, you know that.

A mother is supposed to love her child unconditionally, I know. The parents choose to give birth, not the child. It's the parents. But when the child grows up and ceases to be your own—when the son becomes not entirely "son," not a complete son—must you still love without condition? I know your answer. Mine differed from yours the day you told us. But now I'm not so sure.

The drive was nice and normal that day, a little morning traffic, but not much. As we drove onto that campus of yours, I sat up straight in the car like a little girl in the front seat of a horse-drawn carriage for the first time. I belonged at Arkansas State University—a university —I belonged there because my boy was studying there. So proud. I was so proud driving in, but on the way out, I nearly stuck my head into my big black purse.

Tonight, to precede your favorite cake, I'm fixing your favorite dinner, what you'd call your "Delish Dish," remember? Sautéed chopped meat on spaghetti—no tomato sauce. "Hold the tomatoes!" you'd say, acting like a waitress, like a waiter, in the diner. Always your favorite dish. With mushrooms. I remember. How could I forget? So European. My boy's favorite dinner. In junior high school you used to con me into letting you take a plateful into the den and watch the TV while you ate. You promised you wouldn't spill a drop and you never did. You kept your word. You always were a good boy. A good boy. You are still our good boy. YOU ARE MOMMY'S GOOD BOY. Spaghetti and Superman, your favorite dinner. You may think I've forgotten, but I haven't. Not a thing.

I understand that you can't be here tonight. I really do. But just remember that we haven't forgotten you. I'm fixing your favorites so you know.

How I loved your dormitory building, Delta Hall, a men's residence, a residence for men, for real men, normal men, a long and rectangular and masculine building with yellow brick, all golden in the sunlight like Samson's golden locks ready to be shorn . . . unless his hair was black—Does the Bible say? What does the Bible say? I confuse my Bible lessons sometimes. And didn't you ever learn anything from your old Mom about decorating? Orange curtains over a green shade! And that gold, plastic-framed mirror from Wal-Mart. Made your room look like a den of sin. A hint?

You acted glad for the goodies, and I didn't suspect the least little thing when you told Dad and me to sit down on your creaky, narrow bed. I remember how you pulled your desk chair over and looked us both in the eye, from one to the other, and said, "Mom, Dad, I've got something to tell you. I've joined a group, a student group. The Gay Alliance."

Your old room at home's the same. We haven't changed a thing. Still that royal blue carpet I always called "Hideeeeeous!" Remember? I exaggerated a bit, I know, to make my point. That's me. You know not to take all my exaggerated reactions seriously, don't you, son? And that bright blue burlap bulletin board I sewed for you still hangs over your desk. And all those maps you used to sit and draw and color, all those maps of all those foreign places—Rhodesia and Ceylon and Zanzibar and Manchukuo. I never understood why you couldn't draw maps of America. Dad and I were always suspicious of people from those sorts of foreign countries. How can you trust someone who's so different? Lord knows what to expect.

And that desk Dad built for you out of old plywood pieces and brass handles—still here. By the time we could afford better, you'd grown so used to it you wouldn't hear of our replacing it with a store-bought one. When you were ten, you said you could never work at any other desk but that one because it was filled with nails of magic that had been hammered by Dad's love. He and I just stared at you when you said that. All of ten years old. So sensitive so young. Always full of surprises. That's when Dad decided to take you to Chicago, like a reward for your loving him.

Always surprises. Like the time you nearly gave me a heart attack with that horrible Halloween costume of yours. "Mom, I've got something to tell you." And I turned around—shrieked. I would have sworn on a Bible that someone had plucked out your left eye, that your face was dripping with real blood. Shrieked so loud your father came running in from trimming the lawn, not so much as wiping his wet shoes on the doormat. He gave you a wallop for that one. Remember? I remember. He didn't hit you often, only that once really, when you upset me so. Then that one other time.

You know I'd write if I could. I just can't seem to bring myself to. Not sure what I'd say if I did. Babble, I suppose. About old times. Happy times. Together times.

Remember the time you brought me a mud pie, all gooey and drippy, and I was terrified you'd drop it on the carpet in the living room where you'd brought it to show me, all proud of how you could bake like your mom? Of how you made the pie, since I told you I just didn't have time to bake one. I told you then that sometimes it was better to have no pie than a mud pie. Some lessons you just refused to learn.

"The Gay Alliance," you said, just as though you were telling us you'd joined the glee club or debate society or chess team.

"The what?" Dad spat out. He looked at you all wrinkle-eyed, as though he didn't find your joke funny at all but was trying hard to see the humor.

"The Gay Alliance."

His eyes opened wide. "Why? You think you belong there?"

"Yes, Dad. And I have a friend."

All of a sudden I heard a scream. It was my voice. I recognized it, but I still to this day can't tell you where it came from, that scream. "You're wrong! You're wrong! No son of mine could possibly belong in a group like that!" Then I punched your father in the shoulder. "Do something, Henry! Don't sit there like a lump, do something!"

Dad just stood up and slapped you with the back of his hand, crack across the face, knocked you onto your back onto the wooden floor. When you tried to roll away, he pinned your arm with his foot. Your skinny arm under Dad's scuffed-up Timberlands. Oh, Lord, I remember.

"Tell me you lie," he growled. "Tell me you lie."

"Dad, that hurts! Get off my arm!"

"Tell me you lie." Like a wolf he growled.

"Dad, stop!"

"Tell me you lie!" And he stomped and kicked with those heavy boots of his.

Did you fight back? Did you strike your old dad? No. You were always such a good, respectful son. You wouldn't hit Dad. Not ever. So you only tried to shield yourself from his blows.

"Mom, make him stop!"

And automatically I stood up, and I don't know where I got the idea, but I grabbed that hideous gold plastic-framed mirror off your wall. My empty black purse dangled helplessly from my elbow as I held that mirror high over my head.

"Hit him with it, Mom! Hit him!" You just couldn't bear to hit him yourself.

And I looked at him stomping and kicking and punching and I felt the knife twisting in my breast and I just cracked that mirror down hard as I could.

Right onto your flailing legs.

Twice.

The Lord help me. All I wanted at that moment was to crush the life out of you, out of the hideous monster I'd birthed into the world.

But that was then. I wouldn't want to do that now.

So, how are you managing, son? We're proud of you. Proud of you and love you and pray for you every day.

And how's your—(I'm taking a deep breath here)—your friend? I'm ashamed to say I forgot his name. I guess I never really knew it. Did you even tell me? How is he, that man, your friend? You're still with that same friend, aren't you? I'm so glad you're settled down with one person. Especially these days. Really. I watch TV.

For tonight's appetizer, I opened the fruit cocktail and added those tiny little marshmallows you like. Then I stuck the whole bowl in the fridge so it would get cold, just the way you like it, or the way you used to. We'll eat it and think of you, Dad and I. We think of you all the time.

We all do crazy things when we're surprised. Don't always know what it is we do, what it is we say. I know. . . . You're thinking about what I said. You know I couldn't have meant any of those things. You know I'm glad you were born. The day you were born was the happiest of my life. Nothing I could say afterward could change that. Nothing. You're the most precious thing in my life. In our lives. We love you, son. We adore you. We're proud of you. We're thrilled you've found happiness. We think you're the most wonderful boy in the entire world, and we love you love you love you love you.

Maybe next year on your birthday I'll be able to write to you. Maybe next year you won't have to compose this Happy Birthday letter by yourself, this letter you've stopped expecting from me, this letter you still wish were from me. Thank you for thinking of me, Son.

All my love, forever and ever,
Mom

–5–

A Girl Can Dream

Ed Wolf

I was the tallest, skinniest boy in St. Joseph's School, and I hated the way I looked. My body was so white, so thin, so unformed. When my mom would pile us all into the car and drive over the causeway to Miami Beach, I always went into the water with my T-shirt on. My body was my shameful secret, and I let no one see.

Many years of parochial school had kept this perception intact—had even fostered it. But St. Joseph's School only had eight grades. So one September morning I found myself walking through the long gray corridors of Westward High.

Eight years of parochial school had prepared me academically for Westward. I liked that feeling, thinking I knew more than the others. And the teachers at Westward were more interesting—because some of them were men. The nuns had taught me to read and write, but Mr. Newman had a solid, muscular body and a handsome face. I could see the hair on his arms, the cigarette pack in his shirt pocket; small damp semicircles would form at his armpits as he got excited about algebra. I was fascinated by Mr. Newman, Mr. Parker, Mr. Rich, and Coach Delmano.

It was actually fear that I felt when I encountered the coach. Catholic school had never included any physical education or Coach Delmano. He had a big belly that hung out over his pale white legs, and the baseball cap he wore was too small for his large fleshy face. Our first class consisted of him leading us through the damp boys' locker rooms and emphasizing the importance of "dressing out." This meant changing into shorts and a T-shirt before heading out to the playing fields. He also stressed taking the required shower before going on to the next class. I was horrified at the realization that others would see my shameful body—and that I would be seeing theirs.

As I stood in the locker room, towering over the other boys, one of my classmates slipped quietly in behind the coach as he was illustrating the correct way to dry off with a towel. Someone in the group whistled. Someone said, "Hey, it's Norman the queer."

What I remember most was his long hair. I'd never seen a boy whose hair was as long as Norman's. And none who had hair that shined and moved so perfectly as when Norman turned his head and glared at the boy who hooted, "It's no-man Norman." As the rest of the class laughed, Norman leaned gracefully against a locker and watched the coach pulling a towel back and forth between his meaty legs.

I encountered Norman again the following day in the locker room during our first gym class. We'd been ordered to dress out. I faced the lockers while I stripped down to my underwear and put on my khaki gym shorts. I was so self-conscious, my penis disappeared altogether. As I turned around to tie my sneakers, there sat Norman. His locker was next to mine. He was wearing a pair of bright red underwear and was brushing his beautiful hair with one hand while reading a book with the other. He held the book up in the air in an exaggerated manner, so everyone could see the title, *A Girl Can Dream.*

An older boy came up behind Norman. I'd heard someone call him Jack, talking about how many times he'd failed eighth grade. He had broad shoulders and large powerful arms and legs. He was naked and had hair on his chest, arms, and legs; he had hair sprouting out from under his arms. He also had a large, dark, V-shaped patch of hair at his crotch, right above his thick penis. As I stood watching him approach, I felt a faint tingling in my groin. I quickly looked down to tie my laces.

Jack stepped over the bench that Norman was sitting on and plopped down next to him. "Hey, little girl, whatcha readin'?" He reached for the book in Norman's hand. Norman pulled away quickly and then stood.

"None of your business. And I'm not a little girl!"

One of the other guys got on his hands and knees behind Norman as Jack rose. "That's right, fairy. You ain't no girl!" Jack shouted and then pushed Norman backward.

A circle formed around Norman as he got up. His face was bright red. He picked up his brush and his book and sat back down. I thought he might begin to cry, but he didn't. He calmly found his place in the book and continued to read. After a few moments, he raised his hand and began to brush his hair again.

Jack struck out toward Norman's face and hit the brush instead, sending it skidding across the locker room floor. He grabbed Norman around the neck with both hands and shook him violently. "You queer!" Jack yelled. "You fuckin' queer!"

Norman put his own thin hands on Jack's and tried to pull them off. He made no sound. His eyes moved around the circle of spectators and then settled on me.

I could feel Jack's hands as if around my own throat and I couldn't breathe. Norman grimaced and tried to stand, but Jack wouldn't let go. I could see tears in Norman's eyes as he continued to stare at me. I didn't know what to do.

A loud piercing sound made everyone jump, as Delmano barged into the room with his whistle shrieking. "Let's go, little girls," he called out. "Everyone into the gym." The circle of boys turned away as Jack let go of Norman. "Faggot," he hissed, as he moved away toward his locker.

I wanted to do something for Norman. I thought of sitting down next to him. I thought of picking up his book, retrieving his brush. He sat in front of me and wiped his face with his T-shirt and then finished dressing out. He looked at me again and then left the locker room with the others. I hurried out behind them.

Over the next few weeks, the hour and a half I spent in gym class became the focal point of each day. I was still shamefully embarrassed by my thin gawky body on display in the showers. But I had also discovered the pleasure of discreetly watching the others as they moved nakedly around me.

Jack continued to torment Norman. I heard that he had kicked in the door on the bathroom stall that Norman was using and had pissed all over him. I watched one day as Coach Delmano purposefully matched them up as wrestling opponents and then let Jack twist Norman's arm so painfully that he had cried to be let go.

I tried to say something to Norman that day. Because Norman had started crying on the mat, Coach stopped all the matches and talked about one of his favorite topics—"No pain, no gain." He told Norman to go to the showers before the rest of us. "Pull yourself together, boy," he said.

When I got to my locker, Norman was gathering his hair into a ponytail. He held a pink elastic band in his mouth as he pulled his hair together. We looked at each other. I wanted to say something, but I was afraid to talk to him. He finished dressing and closed his locker door. Someone had written QUEER on it.

The following week, Jack and I were matched up as wrestling partners. Because I was tall and able to stay stretched out on the mat, it was impossible for him to get me on my back and pin me. He scrambled all over my body, repeatedly trying to flip me. All of this physical contact highly aroused me. I was grateful not to be painfully pinned by him, but staying on my stomach also allowed me to keep my bulging erection a secret.

We all entered the showers together. The hot water felt good as it ran down my back, and for the first time, I felt okay about being in this class. So far, I was the only one to have successfully eluded being pinned by Jack.

As I stood by my locker and began to dry off, I watched Jack take his towel and fold it lengthwise very tightly—a rat's tail they called it. He dipped the exposed tip of this roll into a puddle of water and flicked it once. It made a loud cracking sound like a bullwhip. Then he moved toward me.

Norman emerged from the shower and crossed to his locker. He stood between Jack and me, drying off his arms and chest. Jack slowly moved forward. Norman raised his foot up on the bench and began to dry his leg. He was facing me as Jack came up behind him and took careful aim at the pouch that hung down between his legs.

Jack flicked the rat's tail very quickly, and there was a loud cracking sound as it whipped through the air and made contact. Norman jerked forward; his body trembled as something dropped down between his legs and landed softly on the floor beneath him. He looked at me, his mouth open, as his whole body tightened. Then he fell forward with a groan, slamming into his locker door. Jack was staring at the floor, his mouth open, all the color gone from his face. One by one the other boys stopped what they were doing and peered over toward Norman and me.

I came around the end of the bench and saw a small yellow sack lying on the floor. I saw some blood and a blue-black vein that still connected the sack to Norman.

We all stood silently looking at the floor. Coach came in to see why everything was so quiet. He saw Norman and screamed at us all to get out. Norman began to shudder and cried out once, very loudly, and then we all began to move. Lockers were flung open and everyone dressed as quickly as possible. I was standing very close to Norman, but I didn't know what to do. I got my clothes out of my locker and then stepped away from him to put them on. Coach Delmano came running in with a blanket, yelling, "I want everyone out of here now!" and then he covered Norman. I left the locker room with my shoes in my hands.

I wanted to see Norman again—to say something, to do something—but he never came back to Westward. And Coach Delmano eventually found out what happened that day and then Jack was gone too.

I entered the locker room one day and Norman's old locker looked different. The maintenance man had tried to remove the word QUEER, but I could still faintly see the letters if I really looked.

I stood in front of Norman's empty locker feeling scared and sad at the same time. There was only one thing I could do to make what had happened any better. I moved my things into it.

On the top shelf was that book, *A Girl Can Dream*. I took it home and read it. It was about this girl who didn't fit in at the school she went to and how, after a lot of problems, she found a friend. And it eventually made everything different.

–6–

Still Dancing

Jameson Currier

The class begins at 8 p.m.; the room looks remarkably like a minia-ture version of the cafeteria where my high school held its sock hops. I am always amazed at the people who take this class on a Saturday night, a beginner's introduction to country-western two-step dancing sponsored by the Southerners, a social group of expatriate gays and lesbians in the New York City area. The men and women are wildly diverse tonight: ponytails, buzz cuts, tattoos, and earrings. If anything is predominant, it would have to be denim and T-shirts.

The instructor's name is Lori, a tall, handsome woman who in differ-ent clothing could pass as one of Chekhov's sisters, but tonight she is wearing jeans and a sleeveless plaid blouse, her blonde hair twisted into a braid that hangs down her back. She assembles everyone into the center of the room, about fifty of us, and she shows us the basic step—a rhythmic shuffling of the feet back and forth in a quick-quick, slow, slow pattern. We spread out to try the steps alone, but I feel so oddly exposed dancing by myself that I concentrate, perhaps too seriously, on my steps. Beside me a beefy guy with a goatee hooks his thumbs through the belt loops of his jeans and casually sashays through the steps as Lori repeats over and over, "Quick-quick, slow, slow. Quick-quick, slow, slow."

Next we form a large circle and Lori explains that two-step dancing follows a circular, counterclockwise motion around the room. A short black woman with huge, expressive eyes helps Lori demonstrate the dance we will be learning, and then we are paired up. My partner is a lesbian named Judy, and Lori informs us that we must make a decision within our couples as to who will lead and who will follow. (In Fred Astaire ballroom lingo that means someone must dance the boy's part and someone must dance the girl's part.) Judy says succinctly, but nicely, that she would like to lead, and though I squirm a bit, I know it is just my male-chauvinistic reactionary act; I actually want her to lead; so far in every lesson I've had, I have been the leader, and tonight I want to practice following.

Lori offers more pointers: where to place the hands, how to keep the steps going in different directions, how to weave around the other couples. Before you know it, a Bonnie Raitt tune is pumped timidly through the loudspeakers and Judy, amazingly agile, leads me steadily in a dance around the room. Next thing I know Lori is teaching the leaders how to twirl the followers, and as Judy and I work our way through the motions, I have this silly thought racing through my head: this is a girl who likes girls who's dancing like a boy with a boy who likes boys dancing like a girl. When we stop, I pitch my eyes toward the floor, unable to control my smiling.

I am here tonight for several reasons: to conquer my shyness and to escape some frustrations—bills, solitude, the news of a friend who just died. My friend Jon who now lives in California told me he goes two-stepping and has a great time. "Forget cruising," he said, when he first recommended I give this a try. "This is better than disco was in the seventies. And you get to touch someone while dancing." I am a single gay male in his midthirties, but I'm not here tonight to try to meet anyone; still, several men here intrigue me: the sandy-haired man I recognize from a television commercial; the lanky brunet reminds me of an old boyfriend; the guy behind a table of refreshments I will study all night— fair and hunky, dark eyes, great arms, a balding patch at his forehead.

Though I mastered the basic steps a few months ago, I still take the class to practice; I also find it's a way to break the ice with other new-comers. Lori has us change partners and I'm paired up with a guy named Gus, a man I find so good-looking I probably would never speak to him under different circumstances. Dancing with him, I get this crazy, porno-graphic thrill when he shifts his hand from the center of my back to the base of my neck and my hand slips down his shoulder, feeling out the bulkiness of his tricep. Our eyes keep meeting and breaking apart, and I feel myself beginning to sweat, confused as to whether it's from my sudden nervousness or the physical exertion of dancing. I am almost thankful when Lori stops the dancing to teach everyone a simple line dance.

Then suddenly the hour is up; the class is over, and everyone applauds and thanks Lori. But no one leaves the room: the lights are dimmed, the music brightened. The class was only an appetizer; now the main course—The Dance—begins. An awkwardness momentarily descends, everyone looking eagerly from the sidelines at the empty dance space until two guys whom I suspect are lovers break the spell and begin dancing. When I first starting coming to these dances, I hardly danced with anyone, preferring to watch from the side, trying to pick up the steps as the music changed. But one of the things I like most about these dances is the unspoken rule of Southern politeness —that if someone asks you to dance, you do not say no—a rule that has pulled quite an assortment of strangers toward me, and me hesitantly out to the dance floor, cautioning my partner on my inexperience.

Tonight I dance more than I have at any of the other dances I have attended, attributable, I think, to the fact that I am more comfortable and the rhythm of the steps now feels natural to me. Two-step dancing has its hits, like every other style of music, and the crowd swells to the dance floor as the taped music reels through favorites by Dolly Parton, Garth Brooks, Clint Black, Mary Chapin Carpenter, and almost anything by k.d. lang. More and more people begin to arrive—the better, more experienced dancers—and they take to the floor, whirling around the room, making all this motion as giddy as a ballroom competition. I recognize several people I have noticed or met at the other dances I have attended; in fact, I am beginning to sense a regular crowd, those who follow the underground circuit of bars and clubs in Manhattan where gay and lesbian two-step dancing is featured on different nights of the week. Everyone I speak to here tonight seems to find this type of dancing addictive, as invigorating and popular as country music has become.

There are few things I enjoy as much as dancing, an outgrowth, I believe, of being a product of the disco generation. When I was first struggling with my sexual identity back in the seventies, the most important thing a friend did for me was to take me to a disco, introducing me to a world of men who acted, believed, thought, and danced just like I did. Even when AIDS began changing the landscape, I found comfort and solace simply through dancing; by then, dancing for me was no longer a cruising ground for sex; it was simply a physical pleasure, as narcotic and indulgent as going to a gym.

The hours literally dance by; every now and then the dancing breaks into a waltz or a pseudo-square dance called the Cotton Eyed Joe. When the room shifts into the Texas Cha-Cha, a line dance performed to Clint Black's song "Gulf of Mexico," it is one of most romantic and breathtaking moments I have ever witnessed, the choreography merely a simple series of fluid walks and pivots. And then a tall, handsome man asks me to dance. As he leads me to the dance floor, it occurs to me that I met him years ago at a house party on Fire Island. When he introduces himself as Joe, I am convinced it is him, but I do not say anything; I merely place my hand at his shoulder and we begin to dance. As I recall, Joe had a lover back then, a man named Randall, and as we move brightly, swiftly around the room, I wonder if his lover succumbed to the same fate as the friend who accompanied me to all those parties that summer. Joe tightens his grip around my waist and leans in closer; I can smell the sweat of him. Even if he remembered me, he leaves abruptly when the dance is over.

A little later, when I glance at my watch, I notice it is almost midnight, and like Cinderella I decide to leave the ball early, not wanting to break the enchantment. Gus catches me at the doorway and writes his phone number on a slip of paper for me. It makes me feel buoyant and hopeful. On the subway uptown, I wonder if all this dancing, all this Southern country stuff, is a way of finding the roots I left behind when I moved to Manhattan from Atlanta almost two decades ago. In the past few months it seems I have been searching out Southern culture in the city more and more—in restaurants, music, bookstores, even the way I dress—I have adopted an affinity for wearing boots.

Back in my apartment, I'm still dancing, floating through some remembered steps by myself. Quick-quick, slow, slow. Quick-quick, slow, slow. No, I think. It's not the roots. It's in the genes. I just love dancing. It makes me forget a lot of things.

−7−

The Preacher's Son

George Singer

I knew it was dangerous to watch Taylor Haines, the way his blue-glass blue eyes darted, but I couldn't help myself. He was restless, fidgeting in his chair—slouching, bouncing his knee with a scowl on his face. The desks were arranged in a U, and I had a perfect view of him. I'd never seen him in that blue crewneck sweater before. He must have gotten it for Christmas.

The sweater was of a particular cobalt shade that turned his eyes brilliant and tinted his Southern white Cracker skin like fine porcelain. His dirty blond hair, parted in the middle, hung to his shoulders and shone like he had just washed it.

That was the day Taylor Haines caught me staring at him in Social Studies the winter before I graduated high school in 1979.

I had been in love with him for over a year, even though I was still dating girls and was pretty sure I wasn't gay. Taylor Haines's gym locker had been right next to mine my junior year, and each night I had jerked off to memorized glimpses of him in his graying underwear, always ripped at the elastic band. There was a light dusting of freckles on his shoulders and his blond hairless body was all pumped up from his brother's borrowed weights. This was 1979—before everyone got muscles—when most people still just jogged and played tennis and had never even heard of Nautilus.

When the bell rang, I couldn't help stealing one last, longing look. I was already mooning over the fact that I might not ever see him again after graduation.

Taylor Haines looked right at me with those unbelievably blue eyes of his and sneered, "What are you? A fag?" The room stopped. Everybody looked. My head went down, hot with shame. I closed my books and kept my eyes on the floor.

Even though he was only seventeen, Taylor Haines had already lost the freshness of his youth. His eyes were always puffy and he was always in a bad mood. I remembered the cries outside the school just a few weeks ago—"Fight! Fight!" In back of the building, a crowd of kids surrounded one boy in a jean jacket with a Confederate flag sewn onto the back sitting on top of another boy.

It was Taylor Haines pummeling Jimmy Mulberry. His arm went up, then slammed down on Jimmy Mulberry's head. Fast. Relentless. Bam! Bam! Bam!

Mr. Luca, the geometry teacher, broke through and yanked Taylor Haines up by his arm. Jimmy Mulberry got up slowly. His shirt was torn and covered with dirt. His nose was bleeding and one of his eyes was red and already swollen shut. Mr. Luca didn't ask any questions. He grabbed Jimmy Mulberry's arm as brusquely as he'd grabbed Taylor Haines's and dragged them both straight to the principal's office.

Taylor Haines turned back to face the crowd of us and raised his free arm in a victory fist, smiling his infamous chipped-tooth smile. If there hadn't been fresh splashes of Jimmy Mulberry's blood along the sleeves of his jean jacket, you'd have never even known he'd just been in a fight.

When I saw Taylor Haines waiting for me in the hall outside Social Studies, right after he called me a fag in front of the whole class, I thought for sure I'd end up like Jimmy Mulberry. Instead, he showed me his chipped front tooth in a half smile. He raised his arm and I shut my eyes, but he was just pushing a hunk of blond hair out of one eye.

"I'm not gonna hit you," he said, "You're all right, Claysen." Then he sort of patted me on the shoulder and swaggered away.

Taylor Haines's reputation for sexual prowess was legendary in the town of Cooksville, Tennessee. One story told how Walter Ogelthorpe had come home early from work one day to find Taylor Haines in bed with his wife. At the time, Taylor Haines was just thirteen.

Not that anybody other than Walter was surprised about Louise Ogelthorpe. She was working as a Nashville stripper when she met

Walter. And everybody knew she liked to walk around her house wearing only bikini bottoms. If you knocked on Louise Ogelthorpe's door, she just might open it with nothing on her tits. She didn't act surprised or anything. She sort of liked the attention, I guess.

That night after he had called me a fag in Social Studies, I was lying in my bed when I heard a rattle at my window. I leaned up and saw Taylor Haines standing in the glow of the streetlight, tapping his finger on the glass. It was late January and he was shivering in his jean jacket.

I realized then that Taylor Haines must be poor, too poor to afford a proper winter coat.

He was tapping to get my attention and calling me softly by my first name, "Chaaaaarrrlieeee! Chaaaaarrrlieeee!"

I raised the window, hiding my shaking hands. He climbed into the room and smiled at me. I smiled at him, even though I wasn't sure if he was there to beat me up.

"You wanna get high?" he asked.

"Well, okay," I said.

He pulled out a joint. "It's cool, right? I don't want anybody busting in here screaming about the cops."

"It's cool," I said. My parents were sound asleep. I could faintly hear my father snoring upstairs. They would go through the roof if they caught us, but as long as I could still hear my father snoring it was worth the risk.

"Good shit," I said, trying to divert attention from my hands. His gesture of friendship made them shake even more.

"Uh huh," he answered. Then he put the joint out on his sneaker. He reached over and grabbed the back of my neck and pulled me down into his crotch and undid his pants.

Taylor Haines knew exactly what he wanted, and he held my head in both his hands and guided me into doing it just the way he liked it.

It felt like a girl's tit I'd sucked once. All skin. But I got hot. The fires of hell flushed all over me. I could actually see the too-white skin all over my body blotching beet red, even in just the light from the streetlight.

This was what I had been waiting for all my life. But my own sweet fantasies had never quite gotten past Taylor Haines just standing by his locker in his graying, ripped briefs. Through it all, my father snored. I listened, making sure he hadn't stopped.

Afterward, Taylor Haines smiled, "Not bad, Claysen." Only when he wanted sex would he call me by my first name, Charlie. When it was over he would call me by my last name, Claysen.

Even after he climbed out the window, ran alongside the house, and was gone, my hands were still shaking.

He returned every couple weeks, or something like that, always a little drunk. Sometimes he was so drunk the room would stink of it and he'd sway with my mouth on his dick, unable to stand up straight.

I passed him in the hall after that first night and called, "Hey, Taylor," and he sneered at me, "Fag!" I never said anything to him about it when he showed up at my window cooing, "Chaaaaarrrlieeee."

But Taylor Haines wasn't the only boy I had sex with that spring of 1979. There was also Bucky Wallace, a chubby boy with thick dark hair, dotted with moles, and prone to fits of profuse sweating.

People whispered that Bucky Wallace, the preacher's son, was queer. It wasn't just that he couldn't swing a bat to save his life. It was that he *idolized* Lauren Bacall. Once he cried in our English class after returning from a visit to the school nurse because she wouldn't let him go home to watch *How to Marry a Millionaire,* the one o'clock TV movie.

But Bucky Wallace had one thing going for him. His father was Warren Wallace, the preacher of Cooksville Baptist Church. The congregation numbered 600 of Cooksville's measly 2,000 residents. Under any other circumstances, Bucky Wallace would have been teased and picked on and beat up every day of his life. But Cooksville High's all-Baptist football team thought they were somehow closer to God if they sort of looked out for him.

Even though he had a boy like Bucky, or maybe because of it, one of Preacher Wallace's favorite subjects for his sermons was how depraved the *hawmos* were. With a scowl on his face and booming righteousness in his voice, he would go on about Leviticus and Sodom and Gomorrah.

"The *hawmos*," Preacher Wallace told us, "deserve to die a horrible death because of their vile, depraved, and unnatural practices." He would pause, letting this sink in, before he backed it up with exactly where in the Bible his words could be verified. That gave each of his tirades a grave and inevitable credibility. "Leviticus, Chapter 20, Verse 13 *and* Romans, Chapter 1, Verse 32."

"*Hawmos* have the power to create mass intoxication from their wine, which is made from grapes of gall from the vine of Sodom and the fields of Gomorrah. And it is potent enough to poison all the minds of all the little children and all the decent god-fearing Christian people of Cooksville. Deuteronomy, Chapter 32, Verse 32."

The spittle sprayed and his palm pounded the pulpit as he glared and jerked and shook with the righteous words of the Lord's condemnation.

I would avoid his eyes, keeping my head down, certain that all of this was intended for me, for what I'd been doing those winter nights with Taylor Haines.

Once Bucky Wallace sat in front of me during a *hawmo* tirade and began to sweat profusely. The sweat beaded up on Bucky's neck from the power of his father's words—"God himself has forsaken these depraved perverts"—then it trickled down his neck, spreading wet through his shirt, puddling by his pants, until finally it began to drip off the pew and onto the raw pine floor of our church. When the choir started to sing, Bucky Wallace stopped sweating. By the time he stood next to his father on the church steps, saying good-bye to us as we filed out, he was just a little damp.

The spring of our junior year, in the Cooksville High Talent Show, Bucky Wallace did this number from *The Act,* this big extravaganza Broadway show for Liza Minnelli, written by Kander and Ebb. The big Liza showstopper was a splashy number that opened the second act, "City Lights."

I knew all this because Liza had sung it on the Tonys that year and I had watched it. I did not, however, go running down to the Rhino Vinyl record store the next day and order the cast album to be sent down from Nashville and then play it over and over, learning every nuance of Liza's phrasing, as Bucky Wallace must have done.

So while Mrs. Brown from the Cooksville Baptist Church played along on the piano, Bucky Wallace came out in a top hat and started singing "City Lights." But Bucky Wallace didn't just sing it. Bucky Wallace *did* Liza Minnelli. All out. In front of the entire student body and faculty of Cooksville High and all our parents. I blushed for him, in spite of myself.

The way Bucky sang it, the city lights were *SPAHHHHHHHKling,* just like Liza. He sang *Be THEYA,* instead of *Be There,* just like Liza. When he didn't win first place, or any place, he burst into tears and ran off the stage. Even then, he was sort of just like Liza.

Oddly enough, what brought me and Bucky Wallace together was my mother running into Bucky's mother, Eunice Wallace, at the knitting store. Together they decided that I should do some *service* for the church. And by the way, my mother wanted to know, why wasn't I *better friends* with Bucky Wallace? He seemed so nice.

So one Wednesday after school I ended up in the church basement next to Bucky Wallace stuffing the church bulletin into envelopes. We were informing the congregation about the Easter barbecue in plenty of time to put it on their calendars, so I guess it must have been mid-March.

The night before, I had taken a girl, Leigh-Ann, to a party where we drank beer. I liked her and she liked me and afterward we went parking in my 1971 Mercury Cougar XR7 sports car with the black-leather bucket seats that my father had bought for me on my sixteenth birthday for just $800. Leigh-Ann moaned and spread her lipstick all over my lips, but her perfume tasted rank, like chemicals, and I was so limp you would never have known Leigh-Ann was one of the prettiest girls at Cooksville High. I hid my panic and told her I must have had too much beer, although I assured her I was all right to drive. And then I drove her home.

Bucky Wallace was moving right along with the flyers; he already had twice as many envelopes stuffed as I did when he started telling me how all of Lauren Bacall's friends just call her Betty Bacall, which I pretended not to know. Then suddenly he asked me to show him my dick. Right there, in the basement of the church.

I said, "Stopped doing that when I was twelve."

"Wanna see mine?" He asked, then he moved his hand to open his pants.

"No," I said. He stopped and looked at me as if I'd just called him a fag. He started in on one of his sweating fits. Sweat popped out of every pore, and I got an idea of what he was really after. Part of me wondered how it felt for Taylor Haines when I sucked his dick, so more out of curiosity than any real attraction to Bucky Wallace, I undid my pants. I already had a boner.

Bucky Wallace looked around to make sure we were alone; then, just as I'd expected, he dropped right to his knees and gave me the first blow job I ever had. It was sweet and wet and warm and soft, and it let loose in me an explosion I'd have never bet Bucky Wallace, of all people, was capable of causing in anyone, let alone me.

When he was finished, he told me he wasn't a *hawmo* or anything like that. He knew this for sure because he had told God to kill him if he was; then he'd gone to lie on the railroad tracks. He had made a sort of deal with God.

Bucky Wallace's eyes gleamed and his hand went up in a fist toward the ceiling of the church basement, a gesture I knew he stole from Scarlett's vow in *Gone with the Wind.* "If I'm a *hawmo*," Bucky Wallace breathlessly repeated his deal with the Lord, "Bring a train in the next hour. Bring a train to kill me! I would rather die! Crushed! More mangled than Jayne Mansfield! Than to ever have my Daddy find out I was a *hawmo!* Do it for my Daddy, God! Please! Do it for him! Just kill me if I'm a *hawmo!* Just kill me!"

Tears ran down his cheeks. He told me he had lain on the tracks for the next hour staring at his watch, watching the minutes tick by. No train ever came. He told me that must've meant God knew he wasn't a *hawmo*.

I said, "You're not a homo," even though my underpants were damp with his saliva. I always felt so sorry for Bucky Wallace, but I never understood why.

He went back to stuffing envelopes. He didn't say anything at all to me after that. Even when my mom came and I put on my coat and said, "Bye, Bucky," he just kept folding the Easter bulletins and putting them in the envelopes. "Bye," he chirped without looking up.

My mother looked at me like, *What happened?*

"Bye," I said again, feeling like a fool.

I would wait for Taylor Haines every night. I always fell asleep staring at the window, thinking about what we'd do if he came— holding a boner for so long it started to hurt. But I wouldn't jerk off. I wanted to be fresh for Taylor Haines. In case he showed up. Not that he even cared if I came or not. I always just waited till he left to jerk myself off. Then I'd come the minute I touched myself.

I knew he didn't love me the way that I loved him. But he could have anybody in the county, anybody at all, and he came, more than once, to me. I told myself it must mean that he liked me just a little.

One night, early in March, after I gave him a blow job, I tried to get him to hang around a little after, so he could talk to me without worrying about his friends seeing him do it.

"You mind if we smoke some more?" I asked.

"No," he said and relit the joint we had smoked earlier.

"So you gonna hang in Cooksville after school is done?" I asked casually.

"What are you gonna do?" he asked without answering.

I had my whole future planned out around me and Taylor Haines. I'd applied to the tiny University of Tennessee satellite campus right outside of Cooksville and was certain to get in. My SAT scores were just okay, but my grades were impressive. I told myself it all sort of balanced out. I had also applied to the University of Atlanta, basically because my dad went there and he said I had to. I didn't care if I got in or not. My heart was set on the University of Tennessee, where I could spend every weekend back home, in bed late at night, waiting for Taylor Haines.

"Well," I started, "I'm hoping to get into a school close by, so I can still be around a lot." I watched him very closely, looking for a reaction to that fact.

He just said, "Yeah." Then Taylor Haines looked at me warily. "So, you ever done it with anybody else?"

I told him something went on with me and Bucky Wallace in the basement of the church, and he laughed out loud. "Fuck no! The preacher's son?" I thought his chipped front tooth made him look better than any movie star.

"You know, if you ever want to do anything about that chip in your tooth," I said, "My dad's a dentist."

"Oh yeah?" he asked. "Your dad's a dentist? Shit. My dad's in jail. Yep," He scowled. "Fuck."

It was the most he had ever said to me. I wanted to ask him what his father was in jail for, but I didn't. He stood up and went to the window. Taylor Haines was here in my room, opening up to me. I cocked my head to the side and listened as intently as I knew how, hanging on every word.

"My mama died when I was five. My brothers are kind of looking after things. Me included. Nobody's supposed to know. Everybody thinks my grandmother is living with us, but she just collects the checks. My brothers kept my father's roofing business going. We do all right."

I had no idea he was so in need. "That must be tough," I said.

"When June comes, I'm supposed to be up on the roofs of Cooksville and Warren with my brothers. But you know what?" He looked at me intensely. "I'm not going up on no fucking roof for the rest of my life. No, sir. Not me. Did that once and I broke my arm, and I said, 'Goddamn it, never, *never* again!' You know what I'm fixing to do?" Taylor Haines smiled at me. "Go ahead, you can laugh if you want to. But one day, and this is no bullshit, you'll be watching TV and the *Dukes of Hazard* or something'll come on, and next thing you know there's a guy in a deodorant commercial, and you'll say, 'Wait a minute! That's fucking Taylor Haines in that fucking deodorant commercial.' That's right. You will. I am not shitting you either." He laughed and relit the joint. I stared at him. My heart was racing.

I decided right then and there I wouldn't go to the University of Tennessee at all. No, sir. I would go to Hollywood with Taylor Haines and . . . and what? Wash his underwear in the bathroom of some sleazy LA motel?

I remembered that cheesy movie of the week *Alexander: The Other Side of Dawn,* where, like the ad in *TV Guide* said, Alex learns to survive on the streets selling the only thing he owns, his body. I thought about Taylor Haines being like Alexander. I saw him shivering in his too-thin jean jacket with the Confederate flag sewn on the back, leaning against a lamppost in front of an LA bus station at night. I got up and took my blue down coat from off the hook and held it out to Taylor Haines. "Here. Take it."

He glanced at the coat. "Did you shoplift it?"

"No. It's mine. I want you to have it. I'm getting a new one. I was just gonna throw this one away, anyway."

"Throw it away? That's fucked up. You jiving me?"

I shook my head no, and he looked hungrily at the coat I was holding out to him. It was dark blue, all down, and pretty warm.

He yanked it out of my hands and looked it over, like I was selling it or something, before he took off his jean jacket.

The coat fit him fine, like I thought it would. He played with the zippers and found all the pockets like it was new, which I guess for him it was. He looked at me like he was embarrassed because he was so poor. He didn't thank me. He just said, "Well, I gotta get going."

"You want me to throw this away for you?" I picked up his jean jacket, which he'd forgotten about—the one with the Confederate flag sewn on the back. I was hoping he would say he didn't want it and I could sleep with it.

"Naw," Taylor Haines said, grabbing it back. He took a red Tootsie Roll Pop out of the jean jacket pocket, unwrapped it, and popped it deep in his mouth.

After he left, I decided I would try to convince him to come to the University of Tennessee with me. He could even take acting classes.

"What do you mean someone *stole* your down jacket?" my mother asked me from her shiny, white 1979 Buick Thunderbird after school the next day. I had snuck out that morning and returned home coatless with my little tale of woe. She was pulling out of the driveway when I came home from school.

I was shivering. "Well, I left it in study hall and then when I remembered and went back for it, it was gone."

My mother just stared at me. "You know, Charlie, you're going off to college next year. I'd like to think that you're more responsible than that. Get in." She drove me right over to Warren, where they have a big mall, and got me a new ski jacket anyway.

After that, I would see Taylor Haines wearing my old blue down jacket around school. I never said anything to him. And he never said anything to me.

Spring came, and my heart broke, night after night, waiting for him. He just stopped coming. I started to hate myself for having given him my blue down coat in the first place. He must have thought I felt sorry for him being so poor.

The second to last night of high school, he showed up tapping at the window, calling, "Hey, Chaaaaarrrlieeee! Chaaaaarrrlieeee!" He was damp with what at first looked like mud. His eyes were shining. I remember being afraid of him in a way I never had been before. He was agitated and impatient, not slow and lazy, like he usually was.

I held open the window while he climbed into my bedroom. Taylor Haines was covered in blood. I asked him if he'd been in a fight.

"Naw," Taylor Haines said. "I hit a deer with my brother's truck. The fucking deer got stuck on the front bumper, and I had to pull it off and fucking carry it to the side of the road. Thank God the fucking truck is okay. Can I clean up here, Charlie? Please, please, please say yes."

There was a part of me that didn't think it was such a good idea, but I was helpless when he called me Charlie. "Well, the bathroom's down the hall, but my parents are asleep, so just be quiet about it."

Taylor Haines started taking off his clothes. He put them all on the floor in a pile. I couldn't take my eyes off him, and I knew he didn't mind my watching.

Without even thinking about it, stark naked, he opened my bedroom door and strutted down the hall to the bathroom. Somehow, he knew exactly where it was.

When I heard the water running, I went downstairs and grabbed a bottle of Fantastik, a roll of paper towels, and a green trash bag. Blood was smudged what seemed like everywhere. Something was caked on his shoes, and it had all come off on the shiny wood floor. But Taylor was here and he was coming back naked, having just taken a shower. First, I put the filthy clothes in the green trash bag. Then, I sprayed the window frame and floor and bureau until the room was a fog of Fantastik. Then I went through half a roll of paper towels.

I chewed gum to freshen my breath. I wondered if I should take off my pajamas? Yes! Then get back in bed, naked. And hide my boner under the covers.

He came back into my room all cleaned up, wrapped in one of my mother's pink towels that hung on the back of the bathroom door. Taylor Haines wet and clean was astounding, but I tried not to stare at him. I couldn't breathe. He just stood there in the towel and looked at me. I waited.

"I just took the towel off the back of the door. Is that okay?" he asked.

Suddenly, I realized I had better check to see how he'd left the bathroom. My parents would be in there pretty early. So I got up and pulled out some clean clothes I thought would fit him okay and handed them to Taylor Haines. Then, I put on my robe and left him alone to dress.

The bathroom showed no signs of blood because he'd been naked going in. I got my mother another pink towel, closed the shower curtain, and turned the shower off all the way to stop the drip before I went back to the bedroom. It reeked of Fantastik.

Taylor Haines was lying in my bed naked, but facing away from me. "Is it okay if I stay?" he asked, without turning to look at me.

"Sure," I said. I got into bed and turned out the light.

Without turning to me, he muttered, "You're never going to believe it, but today is my birthday. Not that anybody noticed. Not that I give a shit. But I'm eighteen. Fucking today, I'm eighteen."

I didn't know what he meant, so I said, "Happy birthday, Taylor."

I lay there waiting, but his breathing changed and I knew he was asleep. I jerked off, staring at him, careful not to rock the bed. When I was through, I wiped myself clean with a sock. Then, I stared at his back until the sky went pink and I couldn't keep my eyes open anymore.

I awoke to a gasp. My mother was standing in the doorway staring at my bed. Her hand was over her mouth, and her eyes were wide open.

Sometime during those few hours of sleep, Taylor Haines had snuggled up to me and put his arm over my chest. His lips were nuzzled against my neck, and I had a boner.

My mother ran from the room. I was so used to being in pajamas that I just sprang out of bed after her, in a panic. Behind me, Taylor Haines woke up and dreamily murmured, "What's going on?"

I cornered my mother on the stairs. I stood there, out of breath, with absolutely nothing to say. Then I realized I had nothing on, so I tried to cover my dick with my hands.

She had the good sense not to look at me, but she said, measuredly, "Was that another boy in bed with you?"

I couldn't answer her.

She burst into tears. She covered her face with one of her hands and said, "I guess . . . deep down . . . I always knew . . . what you were. What you are." Our eyes met for a second before she looked away again. "I love you, Charlie. Nothing can change that. But you're going to have to be the one who tells your father!"

Tell him what? That I'd fallen in love with Taylor Haines?

She pushed passed me on the stairs before she whirled around and said, "I would never have just burst into your room without knocking, but something terrible has happened to that nice boy Bucky Wallace. They found him this morning in the mudflats, dead. He was murdered. Someone beat him to death. Broke all of his fingers, on each hand. It's horrible. I thought you would want to know." She burst into tears again, turned away, and ran up the stairs.

By the time I got back to my bedroom, the window was open and Taylor Haines was gone—so was the clean T-shirt and jeans I'd given him. But he didn't take the green trash bag of his own bloody clothes. I sat on the side of my bed and stared at what Taylor Haines had left behind in my bedroom.

I remembered the last time I had spoken to Bucky Wallace. It was on the phone one night while my family was eating dinner. I was the one who answered it.

"You're not busy, are you?" Bucky Wallace asked me.

"No. I'm not busy," I said, to irritate my mother, who was glaring at me from the dinner table.

"I want to go see that new Robert Altman movie, *Health*, tonight. I know it's Saturday night and tomorrow's church and all, but Lauren Bacall's in it and it's playing over in Warren, and my daddy says I can even use his car—the one with the preacher's plates. Wanna come?" The invitation spilled out breathlessly.

Much as I'd have liked to have gone to the movies with Bucky Wallace, even thought it would be kind of cool to drive around in the preacher's car, I also knew Saturday night at the movies in Warren would be filled with kids I knew—on dates. I just didn't want to be seen there with Bucky Wallace. "I gotta paper I gotta finish tonight if I'm gonna graduate," I told him.

"Oh, okay. I understand." I could hear the disappointment in his voice, and I wondered if he had been hoping he'd get to give me another blow job.

"Oh, did I tell you I got into a nursing school up in Nashville?" Bucky Wallace said, excited.

I laughed.

"What's so funny?" he asked.

"I can see you wearing one of those little hats."

"They don't make the boys wear the hats," he laughed.

I could have told him about hoping to be at the University of Tennessee, but I didn't say anything at all.

"You gonna be at church tomorrow?" he asked.

"If I finish this paper, I will." There was no paper.

"What's it about?"

"Listen, Bucky, my mom's calling me to dinner," I said and hung up on him.

Every time I saw him in church after that, he just busted out in a sweat and ignored me like we were never friends, which I guess we never really were.

It was Bucky Wallace's blood all over the clothes in that bag.

I could see him lying in the mudflats, bloody, beaten, with all his fingers broken. And I swear to this day I could even hear him crying.

I hid the green trash bag of Taylor Haines's bloody clothes under a folded quilt in an old cedar chest deep in my bedroom closet.

I worked that day at my job at The Gap. Folding jeans that were clean and crisp and not splashed with blood. Smiling and helping the customers. Hiding my growing panic.

"Can I help you find that in your size?"

What did my mother mean she always knew deep down what I was?

"No, we won't get corduroys back in till next fall."

What happened out there in the mudflats between Bucky Wallace and Taylor Haines?

I knew I should have called the police. But I would have had to tell them about me and Taylor Haines and the other nights he crawled through my window, so I decided to keep my mouth shut. At least for now.

Did my mother recognize Taylor Haines in my bed?

I just pretended nothing was wrong. And it worked. The world was exactly the same as it had been the day before. Except for when I started wondering what had kept Taylor Haines from killing me. The new manager, Cathy, came over, looking worried, and whispered, "Are you all right Charlie? All of a sudden you're like real pale."

When I got home, my father was sitting at the kitchen table reading the newspaper, and the table was set just for two, with covered casserole dishes warming on the stove. My father folded the paper, then folded his arms, looked at me, and said, "Your mother said you have something important to tell me."

I braced myself for the worst. "What exactly did she say?"

"Just that you had news. And that I should keep an open mind."

I stalled for time. I needed to figure this out. "Did you hear about Bucky Wallace?"

"Mmmm. Rose Dowell was in today, and you know she works with the sheriff's wife over at the Drug Fair, and she told me that Bucky Wallace was found with his pants down."

This was something I had not heard.

"And Rose said the sheriff's wife told her that Bucky's underpants were twenty feet away from his body." My father shook his head in disgust, whether because there might be homosexuals in Cooksville or because such a senseless act of violence could have happened here, in our town, right under our noses, I wasn't exactly sure.

We began dinner in silence. He looked at me, concerned. He wanted me to start talking. I was the one that always kept the conversation going with my father. But I just wasn't ready to say anything.

He leaned into the table and looked at me blankly. "You're a good kid, Charlie," he told me. "Your mother and I are very proud of you."

I said, "Thanks, Dad." Then I told him I had decided to go to the University of Atlanta. It just popped into my head, but it felt very right.

My father beamed. He reached across the table and grabbed the back of my head with his hand. "Well, hell! I can tell you all about the University of Atlanta," my dad said and busted out laughing, joyfully, with a big hunk of tuna casserole caught between his front teeth. "Now you're talking about my neck of the woods!"

According to the gossip, the sheriff's car pulled up next to Taylor Haines by the ice machine at the Texaco station about seven that night, about the time my father and I were doing the dishes. The sheriff shined a bright light in Taylor Haines's face and started firing questions.

Taylor Haines didn't deny he'd killed Bucky Wallace. He just refused to speak without a lawyer. So they got him a lawyer. Then Taylor Haines said he wanted a better lawyer.

The next day a green Mercedes Benz with Nashville plates pulled up in front of the county jail and out stepped a big fat lawyer wearing alligator shoes and carrying a matching alligator briefcase. This lawyer announced, to no one in particular, that he would be representing Mr. Haines from here on in.

The story spread all over Cooksville like wildfire, and at the end the listener's eyebrow would always arch because never, in all the history of Cooksville, had anyone ever called a Haines boy "Mister."

The next Saturday morning I was still sleeping when my father woke me up, hollering, "Charlie! Phone!"

"Well, hey, Charlie. Now how you doing? You ever heard of Ewell Lee Green? The Nashville lawyer? Well, that's me," cooed the oily voice on the phone. "You know Taylor Haines, don't you? I am actually making this call on his behalf, as he is now my client. Did you know he had a lawyer now? He wants to meet with you. You're not busy today, are you? Say, uh . . . oh, three o'clock? That sound okay?"

It was the first question he actually stopped to let me answer. "Yeah. Three's fine," I said, hiding my fear.

Taylor Haines was waiting for me in a chair at the table in a makeshift interrogation room. In the chair next to him was Ewell Green.

"Thank you so much for coming . . . ah, Charlie," said Ewell Green. "You're doing us a real favor." Then he sprayed a blast of Binaca in his mouth from a tiny aerosol can. "Chili for lunch," he said, with a hearty laugh.

I sat down in the only other chair. I smiled, even though my heart was pounding. I didn't want to be a part of all this.

For the first time in all the years I had been watching Taylor Haines, he had a pimple on his forehead. It was the hugest, reddest thing I had ever seen. Taylor Haines, who was not used to dealing with pimples, had done what every teenager knows you should never do. He had picked it raw. It had festered and scabbed and swollen.

He played with the buttons of his orange jumpsuit. "Hey, Claysen. Thanks for coming." He leaned into me and lowered his voice. Ewell Green stayed back in his chair, keeping his distance. "Listen, if they ask you questions, what are you gonna say?" Taylor Haines wanted to know.

"Why would they ask me questions?" I asked, playing dumb.

Taylor Haines looked surprised and glanced back at Ewell Green with the hint of a smile on his lips. Then he looked back at me. "Come on, Claysen. I have your coat."

I didn't know what to say next. Ewell Green smiled. "Why'n't you let Taylor here tell you what happened over at the mudflats with Bucky Wallace, Charlie."

"It doesn't matter to me," I said. It was the last thing I wanted to know.

"It matters to me," Taylor Haines said. "I want you to know." Then his blue-glass blue eyes looked past me. "I saw him hitchhiking out past Potters Field. He was walking home from a farm that belonged to some lady from his church. I had my brother's truck. I slowed down to pick him up. I mean, fuck, he was the preacher's son. I was just trying to be nice."

Taylor Haines shook his blond head in amazement that anyone could believe anything other than that he was just a good ol' boy, doing a good ol' deed.

He went on, a little sheepishly, "He seemed real happy I even knew who he was." He smiled, embarrassed. Then his face went ugly. "But once he got in and we were driving a little, he started grabbing at my leg. I told him to quit it or I'd make him get out. He still kept at it. Grabbing at my leg and at my dick and trying to put his hands all in my hair and all. So I fucking stopped the truck and I fucking told him, 'Get the fuck out of my truck!' But he wouldn't do it. So I got out myself, and I fucking yanked his door open, then fucking yanked him out, but he fought like a fucking wildcat to stay in my truck. . . . By the time I got him out . . . he was pretty near dead."

"And you just left him there?" I blurted it out.

He tilted his head back, and his eyes turned to slits and he said, "What are you? The fucking DA?"

For the first time since I'd sat down, I was glad Ewell Green was sitting with us because Taylor Haines seemed on the verge of another violent act. Ewell Green's fat hand, the one with the big diamond pinky ring, shot out and rested lightly on Taylor Haines's arm. Taylor Haines willed himself friendly again.

"Look," he went on. "I can't remember what happened. Something went off in my head. It was scary, Claysen. I was scared. Not as fucking scared as I am now, but I was fucking scared. But see, I've just never had another guy put his fucking hands on my fucking dick before. Not a fucking guy. Not ever."

He was lying, of course. But Taylor Haines was gonna try to save his own neck, and he needed my help. This would be the story he'd tell the judge and jury. But none of it would wash if I testified that Taylor Haines liked a good blow job from Charlie Claysen every now and then.

"Sounds like a goddamned pervert if you ask me," Ewell Green said, laughing heartily.

Taylor Haines leaned toward me again. His pimple glistened as he mouthed the word, "Pleeeeeease . . ." He was desperate for my help. He had no idea how little of a threat I really was. I couldn't even drop hints to my dad, so I certainly wasn't about to stand up in court and admit to the whole town of Cooksville that just the *thought* of sucking Taylor Haines's dick gave me a boner.

So I said, "Sounds like Bucky Wallace was a real sicko." I am still apologizing to the ghost of Bucky Wallace for that.

Taylor Haines leaned back and smiled broadly at Ewell Green. Ewell Green let a smile spread over his lips. Taylor Haines looked back at me and said, "And so there was never anything between you and me, right?"

"Other than the fact that you stole my coat?" I asked innocently.

He smiled. I noticed his broken tooth had begun to rot.

"Yeah. That's good, Charlie. We may even be able to use that in court," Ewell Green said, then flicked his wet tongue across his lips.

I suddenly wanted very badly to be back on my bike and on my way home. I stood up. "Good luck, Taylor," I said.

He stood up and held out his hand. "You're all right, Claysen," Taylor Haines said, smiling.

I slapped his palm in a low five on the safety of our secrets.

In the hall outside the interrogation room, I ran into Louise Ogelthorpe. "Hi, Charlie!" She waved real big, and a cloud of cheap perfume wafted over me. She was all dolled up, wearing a ton of makeup and a huge brassy red wig. She was packed tightly into Vidal Sassoon jeans and braless, just about busting out of her shiny purple Capezio leotard, even though she was old enough to be my mother. "Ain't it just awful about Taylor? Poor thing."

She jiggled over to me, a little unsteady on her Candies heels. "I just couldn't let them throw away the key while Taylor, that honey lamb, just rotted away. After all he's done for me? I'm doing all I can for him," she said. Her huge earrings swung as she leaned in to whisper. Through all the perfume, I could smell beer on her breath. "Besides, I know what it's like to be an outsider in this town."

The way she said it made me wonder if she knew about me and Taylor Haines. Then she smiled. "You tell your mamma I said, 'Hey,' won't you, honey?"

My mother would have been offended if she'd found out that Louise Ogelthorpe had asked after her.

Taylor Haines's story of how Bucky Wallace had come on to him and how it made him sort of "go off" was spreading through Cooksville like a bad summer cold. And Taylor Haines was gaining a certain sympathy in people's minds. Taylor Haines was not exactly a fine, upstanding citizen of Cooksville, but everybody knew how Bucky Wallace had been. And everybody believed Taylor Haines's story because of it.

But I was still surprised the morning of the Cooksville Baptist Church's annual pancake breakfast when Preacher Wallace gave his first-ever sermon on forgiveness.

It was a warm, breezy morning in early June. The sunlight had coaxed open the magnolia blossoms, and we could hear the bumblebees buzzing outside the open church door. Preacher Wallace's face softened, and he suddenly looked a whole lot like Bucky. "I'm the boy's father. Of course I want justice. But I know from the scriptures what the Lord wants. That vengeance isn't mine. Vengeance is His! *Vengeance is mine, sayeth the Lord!* So last night I got down on my knees and I asked the Lord, 'Lord put the answer in my heart.' And like he always does, the Lord answered my prayer."

Tears began rolling down Preacher Wallace's fat cheeks. "'Warren,' the Lord said to me, 'What would Jesus have done?'" Now he was crying all out, so bad his sobs choked his revelation. But we still got it. "Jesus would have forgiven Taylor Haines. Jesus would have turned the other cheek. Jesus would have looked at Taylor Haines and seen, here in the middle of good Christian Cooksville, a soul that needs saving. A soul that needs forgiving."

His sobbing stopped, and he became his old, surly self again. "Haven't enough lives been ruined already without us destroying the life of another poor boy who has lost his way?" he demanded of us.

I looked around me. Heads were nodding. A tide was turning. People murmured, "Amen" and "Praise the Lord."

I wanted to stand up and tell the good Christians of Cooksville the truth. That whatever happened out there in the mudflats, Taylor Haines did not "go off" because a guy had touched his dick for the first time. My hunch was that Taylor Haines got Bucky Wallace to suck his dick. Then Bucky Wallace did something that made Taylor Haines go crazy. What, I could never quite figure out.

Even though I could see Bucky Wallace in the preacher's wet eyes, I couldn't stand up and tell my story. It could have been me lying out there in the mudflats, dead, with all my fingers broken and my pants pulled down and no one caring because someone had whispered that I was a fag. But all I could think of was that now no one would ever know about me and Taylor Haines and what went on between us in my bedroom late at night last winter. I wasn't ever going to be singled out for my part. God himself had blessed Taylor Haines getting away with the murder of Bucky Wallace for the sake of the good Christians of Cooksville.

Afterward, across picnic tables behind the church, over pecan and banana hotcakes, everyone said how inspirational Preacher Wallace's sermon had been that morning. But I knew the truth. He didn't want Taylor Haines in court telling everybody how Bucky Wallace had made a pass at him. We were all going to save Preacher Wallace from that embarrassment. And in a roundabout way, we were going to save me from mine.

That same week, a deal was cut with the DA and blessed by Preacher Wallace and his tearful wife Eunice. Taylor Haines was released for time served. I was terrified each night that he might show up again at my window. One night I even thought he had come, but it was just somebody's dog in our garbage. The next day, feeling like I had to *do something,* I buried that green bag of Taylor Haines's bloody clothes in the backyard.

One Sunday later that summer, Preacher Wallace told the church's congregation that he had set up a football scholarship in Bucky's name—not that Bucky had ever been able to throw a football. But that scholarship immortalized Bucky Wallace's manliness in the town of Cooksville for generations to come.

Over a year later, I was sitting in my sophomore dorm room when the phone rang out in the hall. It was for me.

"Charlie!" My mother screamed into the phone. She was one of the few people who still called me that. Everyone at the University of Atlanta now knew me as Charles. "You'll never guess what I heard!" She told me that Taylor Haines was in jail in South Carolina for stealing a car. I wasn't surprised.

I told her I had met someone. "His name is Andy. And I want to invite him down to Cooksville over Christmas break."

My mother paused a second before she said, "I think that would be fine."

–8–

My South

Dan Stone

I never really identified with Eudora Welty's or William Faulkner's South. And Tennessee Williams may as well have been writing about life on the planet Vulcan. My South was a much more succinct and less colorful region, with three seasons in addition to the long hot summer. There were no Big Daddies or black mammies or mint juleps or fat willow trees dripping with fermenting moss, no scandals whispered on verandahs or cats on hot tin roofs, and no lunatic fringe folded and tucked away in the attic.

My South wasn't as steamy or Gothic or romantic as New Orleans or Charleston or Savannah. It was a small world composed mostly of small towns and small churches and relatively small ideas. We had our steel magnolias, but they didn't dress up like every day was Easter Sunday or launch into drawling, outrageous speeches at the drop of a hatpin. I've often wished for a little more of that sort of drama. I've wondered if it might have made things a little easier if there had been a few acknowledged eccentrics or a few bad apples on the tree. Maybe a crazy uncle or two could have taught me to throw a punch, or at least to roll with one.

I was fourteen years old before I even realized that I had a regional orientation. The lessons about individual and group differences began in earnest when my father decided that God was directing him to leave the small south-central Virginia town where he'd been pastoring a Pentecostal church and to transplant the family into a midsize, Midwestern city within a couple hours of Chicago. It was my first extended foray across the Mason-Dixon line, and from the first day of school, I felt as though I had been more or less ambushed.

When the principal at Decatur, Illinois's, Roosevelt Middle School assigned me to my class—the group of eighth-grade students with whom I would be spending seven hours a day for the next nine months—there were no warnings posted. No "Southerners Keep Out" signs outside homeroom. Picture it: 1973. A city best known for its soybean processing and Staley's corn syrup production. A skinny, bookish fourteen-year-old boy in wire-rimmed glasses, just awakening to the hormonal surprise of same-sex attraction, walks into a classroom—a few days after school has started—and is immediately hit in the back of the head with an eraser. Word spreads faster than the spitballs fly that the new kid is a hillbilly. Worse yet, "Jethro" makes straight A's and can't throw a football. No amount of prayer and fasting could have saved me.

For the first time in fourteen years, I began to conceptualize hell as something more than my father's sermons had depicted, something other than a roaring inferno awaiting the end of a wasted life. In fact, hell had a dirty red brick exterior and cracked asphalt surfaces and seven deadly periods that started over again every morning five days a week. And the part about the demons? All true. They punched one another in the face and wrote obscenities on the blackboard and gave the teachers the finger. And that was just the girls.

To say the least, it was an inhospitable environment for a cerebral Southern sissy—an uncivil war zone where there were no gentlemen and no ladies—and where guerilla warfare had clearly supplanted croquet as the primary pastime of the young. My eyeglasses seemed a particularly compelling target for spit wads, and my introduction to the word "faggot" came in the form of barely legible penmanship on a crudely crafted paper airplane that crash-landed regularly on my desk. Self-consciousness was a new phenomenon. Having basked in the benevolent glow of family and teacher approval for fourteen years, I was ill prepared for what I saw reflected in the beady, predatory eyes of this new species. They were aliens whose behavior I could not comprehend, and by comparison, I was a witless, spineless slug in a nerd mask. I was hastily nominated "Most Likely to Get My Butt Kicked," as teachers looked on with vaguely horrified expressions on their faces.

Complicating the struggle was that I was becoming increasingly aware of both mine and other boys' bodies. Finding it nearly impossible to take my eyes off the sculpted, denim-clad behinds of my male tormentors created a conflict of interest few fourteen-year-olds are equipped to manage. The anatomy lessons were the worst, and among the several I was learning was the realization that perspiration could defy the laws of physics—that is, I could experience the effect of sweat with no discernible cause.

The discovery was made in class one afternoon: A cool, rather sudden wetness crept like a spider down my arms and sides. When I made the mistake of investigating, punishment was swift and severe.

"Hey, look, Jethro's feeling his pits!" announced one of the more observant cretins in the vicinity (one whose bottom, I am happy to say, never held my eye). It was about the most titillating spectacle these paramecia had apparently ever seen, and much banter and snickering followed. All I could think to do was to sit perfectly still and wait either for my merciful death or for their limited attention spans to take effect. It was the first in a series of sweaty afternoons, but I'd at least learned to keep my hands at my sides.

"Would you suck my dick for a dollar?" a much cuter delinquent whispered over my shoulder in study hall one morning. The guards let us listen to the radio and Roberta Flack's "Killing Me Softly" was playing.

"No," I replied indignantly. He had hair the color of white corn and long lashes, and he was maturing early.

"What would you suck it for?"

"Nothing!" I said as self-righteously as any preacher.

"Okay then," he winked triumphantly. "Go ahead."

I still remember the burn of that dumb, you-got-me grin on my face. And his name.

Taken out of context, any one of a hundred or so such incidents would have seemed like little more than youthful hijinks—kids being kids. But cumulatively, period after period, day after day, week after week, it took on the feel of cruel and unusual punishment. I was the gift that kept on giving—the ready scapegoat never more than a book or a rubber band or a rock's throw away. I would carry my lunch and, in cold weather, scan the cafeteria for the table farthest from any recognizable faces. When it was warmer outside, I would find empty corners around the building where I could sink into the shadows and steal a half hour's peace.

I've wondered many times since why I didn't fight back, why I didn't tell the little beasts to fuck off or find the nearest projectile and hurl it. The only answer I've come up with is that it was a clash of cultures and my limited coping style. Feeling unarmed and surrounded, I tried to make myself invisible. I would make every effort not to move, to hold my breath, hoping that if I stayed out of sight, I would be safely out of mind. In my South, even in the mid-1970s, decorum still prevailed. Even juvenile delinquents gave lip service to the notion of respecting one's elders. I said "Yes, ma'am" to teachers and went to church every Sunday morning, Sunday night, and Wednesday evening. I played the piano, and my timid soul was unaccustomed to anything but unconditional approval. Good manners and good grades had pretty much provided a magic carpet ride from nursery school through seventh grade. It had never occurred to me that something as natural to me as my accent or the A's on my report card or my tendency not to speak unless spoken to could give offense. No one had ever turned on me before, and I was woefully unschooled in self-defense.

In spite of the trouble it caused me, however, the overachiever's virus that had infected me years earlier continued to rage unchecked. I hid from my classmates. I cried myself to sleep. I got sick most every morning. But my grades never suffered. What's more, I never told anyone what was going on. Not my mother. Not my father. Not even my pillow. Yankee trash might have their weapons, but Southern sissies have their pride. I stubbornly refused to drop my grades so much as one percentile, and I remained as tight-lipped as Tupperware in the face of all the consequences.

Any evidence of my suffering or my nightly prayer for a return to safety surfaced only as an occasional expression of homesickness when visiting relatives back in my mother's hometown.

"If there's such a thing as reincarnation, then I want to come back as a cardinal" (the bird, not the priest), I confided to one of my aunts during a visit.

"Why a cardinal?" she asked.

"Because then I could fly South—back to Virginia" (it's the state bird).

Years later, my South would shrink to several sizes too small. It would grow frizzy and unmanageable as a JCPenney perm. I would complete a long, arduous climb to be free of its humid conformity and its honey-baked intolerance and the distinct drawl that had marked me unmistakably as an outsider. But at that point in my life, my South meant everything hospitable and sure. It meant a grandmother's buttery cake biscuits and sweet potato pie and soft, wide arms; a grandfather's sly pressing of a Kennedy half-dollar in my palm. It meant aunts and uncles and cousins who spoke my language and who treated me like a gift. It was home, and I wanted to go back.

I even made it into a cause, my own private confederacy that I defended in my junior high English essays and journals, arguing to indulgent teachers how Southern states had been constitutionally within their rights to secede, coveting that right as I fantasized regularly about my own secession from the hostile territory I was inhabiting. I started escaping as often as possible from the hard facts of my life into any poems or fictions I could find or create. In the imaginary world to which I retreated, I was a wistful, beleaguered belle clinging to the old days and the old ways, yearning for wide comfortable porches where I could sit surrounded by handsome young suitors—where I was not the ostracized Jethro, but the resourceful and hotly pursued Miss Scarlett.

Of course, no drama with a Southern context is complete without the heroine's inevitable breakdown. Mine arrived unannounced on a day when my mother was picking me up at school for an appointment with the orthodontist (Jethro also wore braces). It had been a traumatic morning. I had unwittingly managed to rub one of the more aggressive female fauna the wrong way. I think I may have allowed my eyes to meet hers. Whatever the offense, it provoked an unrelenting verbal assault—severe even by wartime standards. When the teacher stepped out of the room, the conflict escalated, and the young she-devil moved quickly to my desk and began repeatedly slapping me in the back of the head. Even when the teacher returned, the taunts continued.

I suppose a hardier soul would have disarmed the little heifer or played the good sport. I, on the other hand, had never been given permission (or perhaps, balls) to use force, and I hated sports. I just sat there, flinching, and when I got into the car where my mother was waiting to take me to the orthodontist, I collapsed into six months' worth of pent-up hysterical, dry heaving sobs. We drove straight home, and after calming me enough to piece together the story, my mother phoned the principal's office and, in her sternest "If I weren't a lady" voice, delivered the message that I would not be returning to school until we'd been assured that I would never set foot in a classroom with "those hoodlums" again.

Later we learned that I had been mistakenly assigned to a class of notorious underachievers and troublemakers. There was talk of police records. I was personally escorted by the vice principal to my new class, where I spent the remainder of our stay in the Midwest in a more civilized group of my peers, trying to pretend that the previous months had been a bad dream. I stopped having to dodge missiles. I stopped eating lunch alone. But I would often find myself following a former tormentor down the hall, my eyes focused like two tractor beams on his tantalizing behind.

Several years later, I would spend my first night of quaking, adolescent passion with a lanky, red-haired boy from the Midwest. It was hardly screwing the enemy, but there was a certain closure to it nonetheless. Even now, when I think of the events in my life that I regard as having truly changed it, I always seem to end up back in Illinois. Clearly, I survived the initial trauma of that brief transplant, but although we returned to Virginia where we seemed to belong, the short war had taken its toll. The landscape of my South was forever altered, and the long period of my reconstruction had begun.

– 9 –

Entertainer of the Year

J. E. Robinson

In a crowded and busy supermarket, the most oppressive noise is a young woman yelling for her crying baby to be quiet, or else she will knock her head off. She got everyone's attention.

"You wonder how some people get to be parents," I say to the checker.

"Yeah," she says, weighing my tomatoes. "Tell me about it. Try standing here all day."

For a minute, I feel sorry for the checker. Then, I feel sorry for myself because I work at the Public Aid office and I have seen that young woman before. Without trying to sound the bigot, she is the sort of thing having kids these days, and it is always the kid who suffers most. There is not a caseworker in our office who would not want parenthood to be licensed, to put an end to that nonsense.

Although I have seen that young woman before at the office, and we in the office are sworn to disclose abuse, which her yelling clearly is, I choose not to intervene. Dealing with that mess from 8 until 4:30 gets tiresome, and I have found it best to leave interventions from 4:31 p.m. to 7:59 a.m. to the amateurs. Let them be cursed out and spat upon for a change.

Besides, I have Thelma's groceries, and she is waiting. With the same tact, I choose not to flirt with the baggers, which startles them, I think, because I always flirt. Rarely does it matter with whom. If he is cute and remotely legal (he must be sixteen to work, after all), I flirt. A smile, a compliment, small talk. For the new boys, it is my limp that gets them talking.

"Why you limp?" one bagger asked. "You're too young to limp."

"Yes, I am," I said. "I got one of Noriega's bullets in the butt."

It was just a graze, nothing serious enough to ruin desk jobs and sex, but good enough for a Purple Heart and a couple points extra on the civil service exam as a wounded combat veteran. Never mind it was only a little police action in Panama. The fact is, I feel better walking funny, with a limp. It is a natural for picking up men.

I suppose it was my limp that took Thelma in. "You look like a kicked puppy," she says today, helping me into her house with the combination of her and my groceries. All I can do is grin, for she always calls me a kicked puppy. Maybe it is because at one time I was.

You see, in spite of my bravura, I am fragile in relationships. Easily hurt, I have low self-esteem when it comes to dealing with other people romantically. As the Russians sometimes believe, it is hard to keep the true character hidden.

Thelma called me at work this afternoon for two things: first, to invite me to dinner and, second, to fetch a few things. In other words, she wanted to show me something. I should have known it was just a ruse when I enter her house and smell lasagna baking. A bad sign for relationships, lasagna. Whenever she invites me for a blind date, the smell is always lasagna. It is not that bad all the time. Thelma makes good, romantic lasagna. Thelma is a good cook in general.

"Smells like you started without me," I say. She just smiles and takes her groceries into the kitchen.

"Bruce, I'm just so glad you made it," she says, halfway into the kitchen. "Hard day at work?"

"Work is always hard," I say. I hang my jacket in the hall and follow the smell.

I have been in Thelma's kitchen dozens of times since her son Ronnie died. My first time was the day of his funeral, when some friends and I came over to pay our respects. At the time, we didn't know Thelma— hell, we didn't know Ronnie that well, aside from the days we delivered food to him, when he was in the last stages of the disease. We assumed Ronnie's family had abandoned him, as some do the youngest sons, in some socioeconomic circles. That was why we went to the funeral. We went to Thelma's afterward because dumping proved not to be true in Thelma's case. In her case, she was at Ronnie's bedside until the end, or so the eulogist proclaimed. We just missed her.

As I said, I have been in Thelma's kitchen dozens of times. It smells like my mother's. In fact, it smells better than that. My first time in her kitchen, I was so taken aback that a mother's kitchen on her son's funeral could smell so delicious. Never mind that the food was brought to her by the mourners (I brought green bean casserole). The whole place smelled as though everything had been cooked there.

Usually, Thelma has the dining room set for dinner by the time I arrive. Rarely does she make me eat in the kitchen. Today, for whatever reason, she has us set for dinner on the sunporch out back. And she has a third place set.

"Are we having company?" I ask.

"I hope you don't mind," she says. "Really, he seems like such a nice young man."

How many times have I heard that before? Too many, particularly from Thelma. Among the other benefits of our friendship is her tireless quest for the right man for me, which has been fruitless because her men have been too black and/or too sissy and/or too old, when I like my men rugged, young, and white. I sit at her sunporch table, dreading yet another rendezvous with some coal-black aging she-male named Tyrone.

"Who you got now?" I ask. Thelma is much too busy in the kitchen to hear me. I give up hoping to find out who this new third wheel might be until a tall, clean-shaven, handsome gentleman comes to Thelma's back door. A little stunned, I go to let him in.

"Child, you walk like you done bent over for a two-foot thang," he says through the screen.

Who is this Negro? Not only did he just lay eyes on me, but he is also not even in the house yet, and already, unfamiliar, he is talking about my walk, or something, as though we have known each other for years. I look at him hard. He seems not the least familiar, though he strokes Thelma's geraniums as though he has been doing that for years. At first, I think he is a member of Thelma's family, a run-of-the-mill cousin I met at the funeral one hot second. He does seem to favor Ronnie, even on his sickest days, but we all look alike, you know.

"Thelma," he calls out, crossing his arms. "Miss Thelma! Your downstairs boy ain't letting me in!"

Tittering, Thelma comes to the back door. "Good gracious," she says, "you two met! You two have so much in common, I wanted to introduce you."

What did Thelma think I had in common with that? Aside from breathing? I look at her. She went back to mashing garlic into garlic bread. That left me with this guy, who looks at me like a hungry dog eyeing sausage in the butcher's window. After this guy came in and sat at the table on the porch, I ran into the kitchen.

"What am I supposed to do with him?" I whisper to Thelma.

"Play backgammon with him," she says in a regular voice. "What do you mean, what are you supposed to do with him? You both are my guests. Let me worry what to do with both of you."

She shoos me back onto the porch, where this guy sits smiling broadly. For anything else I could say about him, he does have a handsome smile. And something about him says I saw him before.

"You must be Bruce, Miss Thang," he says. "Hi, I'm Jerry. Fly me."

"I'm so glad you two met," Thelma says from the kitchen. "Now that you two have met, you can just entertain each other so I can finish dinner."

We sit at the table on the porch. What is there for us to talk about? Surely, Thelma must have given it a little more than some thought. "Miss Thang" Jerry, who wants me to fly him, is a little out of his league. I keep shifting my weight because the chairs are a little uncomfortable for my behind, and Jerry decides to make this a conversation piece.

"I see you doing that little hot tamale dance, Miss Thang," Jerry says, "but it ain't got no beat. You listening to something that ain't got no beat, or what?"

"As a matter of fact, I am," I say. "All the rhythm's been bred out of my family."

"Miss Thang" Jerry cannot control his laughter. He gets such a belly laugh he almost falls out of the chair.

"Miss Thelma," Jerry shouts, "now, when you invited me to dinner tonight, honey, you didn't say nothing about Miss Thang, here, having a funny bone. I just got so tickled, I don't know what to do with myself."

"Why don't you just play," I say under my breath. But Jerry hears me and starts laughing again.

"Miss Thang, Miss Thang, Miss Thang," he says between laughs. "Now, girl, you too funny! Now, quit!"

I cannot do anything but shake my head and hope this happy pill he has taken wears off.

Thelma finally comes out carrying a large tray with plates and a bowl of tossed salad. I try playing the gentleman, but Thelma insists upon playing hostess and accepts no help; "Miss Thang" Jerry is happy letting us fuss over who will serve him first. Thelma unloads the plates and the tossed salad. The tossed salad goes to the center of the table, where it sits while she scoops out servings with tongs.

"I'll have the house dressing," Jerry says, trying to be cute. Thelma smiles a little and nods. Out of her apron pocket, she produces a bottle of ranch dressing, which she shakes and hands to Jerry. "Oooo," he croons, "creamy! My favorite. Miss Thang, you like creamy, too?"

I just look at him as if there were precious little he could say that would be more gross and suggestive than that. Thelma, who also chooses not to dignify that disgusting comment, goes to the kitchen for the rest of dinner. She returns with fresh garlic bread and piping hot lasagna. The mix of Italian sausage and oregano and basil makes my mouth water. Then she unties her apron and sits at the table.

Protocol dictates ladies first, but either this Negro had horrible home training or he thinks he is really a female. "Miss Thang" Jerry serves himself first. He takes a hunk of lasagna from the serving dish, spinning the spoon twice to get the last string of cheese. Afterward, he leaves the spoon in the dish. I hand it to Thelma, and she says, "Thank you."

"Jerry," Thelma says, serving herself, "Bruce is from Marshall, Missouri."

"Marshall, Missouri. We practically from the same hometown," Jerry says. He pauses as if he were saying grace, but he is really sucking his teeth before eating. "Girlfriend, you's from the *deep* South. As cultivated as you be, I thought you came from some place like New York City. Thought you done got over here to East St. Louis and found yourself so in love with the Mississippi River, you just had to stay."

"Jerry's from Moberley," Thelma confides.

Great, "Miss Thang" Jerry and I have at least one more thing in common! Maybe we can spend the rest of dinner comparing notes! Hopefully it creates a different talking point than my behind.

"Originally," Jerry says between bites, "I'm from Moberley. Now, we call that the South, but where you from, it's called the '*deep* South.' But, you best call it different, Miss Thelma. I ain't from Moberley, actually. I was just born there. Raised in East St. boogie Louis, though. What did you say you do?"

"I didn't."

"Bruce works for the Department of Public Aid as a caseworker," Thelma says.

"God, that is thankless work," Jerry says. "Miss Thang, my mama worked for the Department of Public Aid all of one year, and after that, she retired to the Department of Corrections. She said, after working for Public Aid, working in any prison is heaven."

Strike two, for another thing we have in common. "What do you do?" I ask, for conversation's sake.

"Me? I just work for the county library on the other side of the river. I am what they call a 'coordinated specialist.' Don't ask me what that is; they haven't even figured it out yet. I like it because it frees up my nights."

"How's that?"

"Jerry's this year's entertainer of the year," Thelma says.

"Entertainer of the year," he says, lifting the tub of margarine to pass to Thelma, "is female impersonator of the year. Every year, the entertainer of the year has an act. My act is that of a cabaret singer."

With that, he begins singing a George Gershwin medley. As he sings, the image comes back to me. Jerry's high cheekbones done in a dusky autumn rouge and his eyes painted light blue. Jerry wore a wig, of course, and stiletto heels. A long sequined slit rode up his leg, as did a beautiful blue gown. Amazing how much you can recall just by hearing someone sing. But it does create a little bit of class in an otherwise classless she-male.

"Were you at the drag show at Magnolias?" I ask, shifting my butt to the other cheek. I begin wishing I had brought my own cushion.

"'Drag show' is such an unkempt phrase," Jerry says. "We just call it 'the show.' Makes it neat and upbeat. Family from Marshall?" Jerry asks.

"Just me and friends," I say. "You?"

"I'm one of ten children," he says. "Not meaning to sound like a cliché, but I am the sissy in the family."

"Do they know about your act?"

He seems slightly offended. " 'Know?' Miss Thang, they *help* with the act. I've got two sisters who are my dressers, another does my nails, a brother that is my arranger—I call him my 'musical director'—don't that just give a fancy touch—and another that drives me when there's an appearance to make. Let's see," he pauses to count, "that makes it five out of the other nine involved with the act, six out of ten, if you count me."

"And the other four?"

"The other four," he huffs. "They're just lazy Negroes. They come so late for dinner, they put CP time back another half hour. Just trifling Negroes. But, I guess that's the same everywhere else in our community."

From the way he talks, a couple of his siblings might be in my caseload. If they are, he doesn't belabor the point. He smiles on the comment, as though he is making a funny. But, no sooner does he do that then he waves the smile off.

"Let me just leave those Negroes be," he says. "Working for Public Aid, you probably get your fill of trifling Negroes. You must go to the Down Under Room at Faces to get away from them."

The Down Under Room at Faces is famous throughout the Midwest for its fantasies. Men go there, and they don't care about their partners. Even the curious wander through. Most are from St. Louis County, crossing the river into Illinois to forget their wives and girlfriends. On any given night, Fourth Street is impassable for all the cars, and you drive on Missouri and Broadway at your own peril. Most would not be seen alive in East St. Louis, if they can help it. For us East St. Louisans, Faces is for the tourists. I give "Miss Thang" Jerry a skeptical look.

"Don't look at me like that," he says. He turns to Thelma. "Tell him, Miss Thelma: if he goes to the Down Under Room, that ain't nothing but his business."

I look at Thelma. I know she has no clue what happens at Faces. I smile.

"Come on, Jerry," I say, "that's low, dragging Thelma into this."

"No, I'll tell you what low is. Low is you going down there to delight in your snow habit." He starts to laugh. "Oh, honey, never mind me. I just look at you and think, 'Sister, you got snow queen written all over you.' I can tell you sure do like going to Belleville to do your shopping 'cause you like eyeing those little white grocery boys. And, on top of that, you are so conservative, Miss Thang, you probably voted for Ronald Reagan a couple times."

"I fail to see what politics has to do with it," I say.

"Oh, Miss Thang, politics ain't got not a thing to do with it. But you did vote for Ronald over my man Jesse, didn't you?"

I do not answer. I just look at him.

"I take that as a 'Yes,'" Jerry says. "But that's okay. I got nothing against Ronald. Any man that can keep this country messed up while battling old timers is all right by me."

Thelma returns with dessert, cheesecake, which makes Jerry's day.

"Thank you, thank you, oh thank you, Mama Thelma," he says enthusiastically. He kisses her cheek. "Cheesecake is my favorite. Is it nonfattening?"

Thelma looks at him as if he were crazy. "Is cheesecake ever nonfattening?"

"Thank you, thank you, oh thank you, Mama Thelma," he says, with the same enthusiasm as before. Again, he kisses her cheek. "Non-nonfattening cheesecake is *always* my favorite!"

By now, I am beginning to wonder where Thelma found this guy, who seems to have a little more life than her usual suspects. Thelma, though, just laughs at his enthusiasm and dishes extra cherries onto his cheesecake.

"Don't you know cheesecake will ruin your figure," I say playfully.

"Honey," Jerry says between bites, "there ain't nothing this cheesecake can do to my figure, except enhance it, as far as I'm concerned."

For some reason, I can imagine Jerry in his shimmering blue dress and bright red boa (for some reason, I can see Jerry wearing a boa), out of shape, from all that cheesecake, and there goes the cabaret family act. Few things are sadder, I think, than an out-of-shape drag queen act.

Finished, Jerry sits back in his chair and pats his stomach. "That was so good, I think I could belch," he says, sounding grotesque. On first sight, I thought he had a little too much class for that, but I end up right anyway, and he just smiles as if to say, "Got you going, didn't I?"

Thelma, in her primness, just smiles.

At this point, sitting is about all I can take. I stand for a minute.

"I was just wondering how long it would take you to do that," Jerry says.

"To do what?" I ask.

"Stand up. You know, Mama Thelma told me about your little war injury," Jerry says. "Being shot in the butt has just gotta hurt."

"Every time I sit up," I say. I sit back down and smile. "It feels better to stand up for a few seconds."

"What was that," Jerry says, "a few seconds standing up every few hours for a Purple Heart? Talk about cheap."

"Eat your cheesecake," Thelma says to him, and "Miss Thang" Jerry does as he is told. He eats the cheesecake daintily, taking bites so small, with his finger in the air, like eating was going to poison him. When he finishes, he sips a glass of iced tea and suppresses a burp. I finish as well and prepare to get going, leaving "Miss Thang" Jerry at the table.

"Thank you for dinner, Thelma," I say at the front door.

"What do you think of Jerry?" she asks.

I shake my head and frown disapprovingly.

Thelma shrugs. "I tried."

We say our good-byes and I leave with my groceries, still thinking about Jerry in his wondrous boa, and still set on wondrous young men.

– 10 –

Hometown

Walter Holland

In the summer of 1979, I went back to the small town in Virginia where I grew up. I was not "out" to my parents, nor anyone else in the town. I had kept my life in New York after college sketchy and secretive. Years in New York City as a dancer and an office temp had produced mixed results. Finally, in late June 1979, after a bad split with my boyfriend-roommate, I was forced out of my apartment. Frustrated and low on cash, I boarded a train south.

For the first month of my return, I stayed with my parents in their small condominium. I looked for an apartment and found one on a tree-shrouded street, a small, straight, residential neighborhood off of an old and elegant southern avenue. My new home was the upstairs story of a once grand, southern "summer house." My view was of the garden in the rear. The small, private terrace entrance at the side of the house had a trellis of wisteria vines and rows of flowerbeds. When I moved in, everything was in full bloom.

In late August, I went to the local college and signed up for courses. My parents loaned me money for school as well as the use of their second car. In September, I began classes with students ten years my junior. My life consisted of the short drive back and forth to the college and a monk's existence with my piles of textbooks and chemistry homework in the quiet upstairs apartment. At night, I took walks along the avenue to escape the boredom and absolute solitude of my apartment. I discovered again that Southerners consented to be pedestrians only at certain times of the day; otherwise, they stayed inside their sensible minivans or sporty Toyotas. The only "sanctioned" stroll was the one done just before dinner at the end of a long, summer day. These walks were taken mostly by matronly women or young housewives who wore bright, white sneakers and pastel-colored sweat clothes. Men were never seen to stroll. The only men I saw on the avenue were runners or joggers. After 7 p.m. or so, except for the rare, bright, long evenings of summer, my frequent walks were seen as an oddity. Used to fifteen years of hitting the pavement in New York, cruising at all late hours, the solitude was both a pleasant change and a terribly isolating experience.

My sister and her husband paid a house visit. My brother-in-law was immensely impressed by my bachelor status. "You'll nail any girl at the college—any girl. Great place you got here," he said obliquely to me as he took his leave. He gave me a grin. I tried to smile.

My life became that of a voyeur. My landlords, the elderly couple downstairs, seldom invaded my private world. They were new to the etiquette of having a tenant. Through my upstairs window and from my frequent strolls, I became familiar with the neighborhood. I knew the woman up the way who was called "Cousin" by my landlord and spoke in a very loud Southern drawl when she came by at four in the afternoon for her scotch.

The street seemed to hold its share of young southern straight professionals stranded in the lonely affluence of the New South. The young wealthy married couple next door had two toddlers, a boy and a girl. They appeared set on transforming their home into a showplace from *Southern Living.* I was struck by the loneliness of the wife, who appeared to dote on her children with ferocious need. One weekend, I observed her hosting a birthday party for a crowd of four-year-olds, replete with a giant piñata suspended in a nearby oak tree, a catered lunch, a clown, a bluegrass band, and enough party favors to decorate two acres of prime backyard real estate.

Afterward, I watched as she sat on the deserted lawn staring for an hour at the empty halves of the piñata. Her husband arrived much later under cover of darkness.

In a starter-upper up the block, a frustrated young housewife-artist lived with her banker husband. I would see her sketching and painting in an upstairs bedroom at night, her husband in his easy chair reading the newspaper, the nightlight glowing eerily from her baby girl's bedroom, the front porch littered with toys.

Beside them, next door, were the two married college professors who entertained all the time and had decorated their house with London theatre posters as well as framed Agnes Martin minimalist prints. The couple ordered books by mail. I frequently saw the packages sitting in their mailbox. They ostentatiously displayed their empty wine bottles on the side porch, I assumed, as a telling reminder of their cultured ways. All the other neighbors were mysteries to me, hidden behind late-day blinds and perfectly manicured lawns.

Everyone knew me only as the "doctor's son" who had come back from "up North" under "difficult to explain circumstances." I felt like David Bowie in *The Man Who Fell to Earth,* an alien creature, fallen as I was from the wild life of New York. I saw my circumstances as only temporary, however, and was convinced that in a short time I'd pick up where I had left off, before money and a bad love affair had set me low. A confirmed urbanite, I persisted in buying *The New York Times* at the local newsstand even though it sold at a hefty price.

I was convinced that gay life, as I had known it in New York City, was nonexistent in Virginia. On my walks, I would slow down in front of the yellow Victorian house of a college drama teacher who had been rumored to be "queer" when I was growing up. I contemplated ringing his doorbell but wasn't certain what I would say if he answered. Sometimes, I found myself bantering on about the City and its ways only to find my "audience" of young college kids or aging local Southerners listening as though I were some war veteran telling tales of former glory. Little would they have suspected the sexual battles I could have described and the huge body count.

Southern days were lyrical and slow, just as I remembered them. Saturdays, I would often go to my parents' apartment for dinner. I was respectful, editing carefully what I reported about my past, mindful of my second-class status as the "failed" prodigal son. My Southern sister, the supermom, had deemed to tell me, in the middle of the Kroger's grocery store one afternoon, about the mess that I had made of my life, how everyone worried about me, and that she prayed I would find a new career and "get myself together."

The Kroger's was my weekly stop for food and an excuse for taking an extra drive across town on an evening. Next to it was the Dixie Laundromat where I cleaned my clothes. The Dixie was a bland concrete building with a plain glass front. On any given day it was frequented by an assortment of Southern humanity: young country couples with their loads of dirty kids' clothes; nervous, thin ladies who chain-smoked and read *The National Enquirer;* even an army veteran with his tattoo and nylon tank top, torn jeans, and motorcycle helmet.

At the Dixie one Saturday afternoon, I was drying a load of laundry when a very cute, blond-haired guy wearing jeans walked in with a sack of clothes. He had milky skin, a nice build, just the trace of a light beard, and he eyed me five or six times. At first, I thought he was smiling toward someone else, but his look registered "I am interested" in so strong a fashion that I realized it had been ages since I'd used my gay radar; it was a little rusty. Finally, he asked me to borrow some detergent. From the quality of the bedspread and sheets in his laundry basket, Perry Ellis and Laura Ashley design prints, I knew that he wasn't a hundred percent "hick."

"You come here often?" He asked. I had to laugh at this cliché and its strange contrast with our present circumstances. An elderly woman smoking Virginia Slims sat next to us on a red-lollipop-colored plastic seat. She hardly listened to our nervous, cruisy conversation.

"I just returned to town. I grew up here but moved away. Now I'm back."

"Well, what you see is what you get," he replied, shoving some jeans and a denim jacket in the machine. What I saw as he moved was appealing after three months without sex. His stretch cotton T-shirt was too small for his body and rode up, revealing a strongly defined, milky-smooth stomach and the tops of his boxer shorts, which had the Calvin Klein logo stenciled on the rim. His "Smith's Feed Store" cap lent him a certain rough-trade look.

"Have you heard Michael Jackson's *Off the Wall?* It's really good," he explained. "You should see the video, too." He gave me a suggestive smile, then told me about the new mall in town where he goes to buy his music.

He took me out to the parking lot and showed me his red sports coupe. He turned on the engine, and the tape player blasted out an array of rock music. The car had the air of a bachelor's lair. A plastic workout water bottle in the cup holder near the dash hinted that he belonged to a health club. In the backseat were a light sports jacket, two pairs of sunglasses, some suntan lotion, and a Burger King bag. I could smell his Aramis cologne. I studied his smooth lips as he spoke, his voice revealing a slight Southern drawl. His jeans hugged his thighs and showcased, when he sat, an agreeable, large bulge. We sat in his car for a half hour or so under the hot afternoon sun until our wash had finished.

We decided to have dinner that evening at my place. Bringing someone home to my tiny room, nestled in the heart of Southern civility, at the ripe hour of seven on a Saturday night, was a totally new experience for me. The dinner went off passably well. My date told me that he worked for the local nuclear reactor plant checking employee safety tags for radiation exposure. I didn't even know there was a nuclear reactor in the vicinity, let alone that this country-looking lad would be handling such a job.

Flirtatious during the meal, I was struck by my new friend's lovesick expression as he cornered me in the kitchen. One bear hug, of sorts, was followed by a powerful kiss. Touching his bare, warm waist under his T-shirt, I was overcome by the feel of the smooth contours of his soft, muscular, trim waist, met in the middle by a dimple. Stripped and rolling around on the floor a few hours later, "radiating" all over each other in ways I hadn't thought possible, I feared making noises in the house where I had lived so cautiously, but soon I threw off all my inhibitions. I lapped at that milky white body and devoured all its young, bulky tenderness. He was in perfect form. Every curve of his sturdy back and butt was a turn-on. Prone beneath me, I rode him, his body traced by red marks from my firm grip and amorous gymnastics.

After he left, I sat in the moonlight of my quiet upstairs room and realized the extent to which I was out of touch with my desires and feelings. The self-imposed celibacy of the past few months and the sort of straight façade I had adopted toward my landlords, the neighborhood, and my college classmates fell away with one touch of his body, one tug on his warm cotton briefs. His large, meaty, clean-shaven cock and balls kept me yearning for days.

A week later, I visited his townhouse, situated in the middle of a newly built development. The living room featured a weight bench, and the dining room, bone china and figurines from Spain. A large, framed poster of Richard Gere hung on his bedroom wall. His upstairs bedroom sported a bed with drawers filled with male porn magazines. He lived a full gay Southern bachelorhood that I couldn't help but admire. Everywhere were the trappings of healthy sexual freedom, but as he got to know me, he shared some of the difficult times he'd endured as well.

At an early age, he told me, he'd been abused by an uncle who liked to play games with him in the bathtub. The abuse had ended short of his sixteenth birthday when they'd both been found out. The uncle was never seen again. Now my friend supported his mother and was a respected success in the family.

He worked the late shift at the plant. It was not uncommon for him to meet his friends at six-thirty in the morning at the Howard Johnson's for breakfast. That Sunday, he was going to a gay social sponsored by the local Gay and Lesbian Hotline. He asked if I wanted to attend. I agreed. He told me the hotline had just started three months ago.

At two in the afternoon, we drove through the impoverished streets of the old downtown area. This was the very same neighborhood where, as a boy, I had gone with my father to get my hair cut by an elderly black barber who had one of the few remaining businesses in the middle of the failing district.

This was a historic area, although funds were limited. For years, its large mansions had been occupied by welfare families, sometimes three or four to a house. Madison Street was cobblestoned and bordered by trellises and gated grillwork. Huge houses with ballrooms and conservatories sat ensconced in the remnants of azalea gardens and boxwood hedges. Some of the homes were weathered beyond recognition, their quarried stones and carved porches coated in soot. Two women, a lesbian couple, had been the first to buy in the late 1970s, setting off the gentrification.

At one corner stood the General Early Apartments, a shabby, red-brick five-story house that provided a home for itinerant men—mostly winos, veterans, and elderly widowers. The neighborhood stayed basically quiet at night; by day its routine was broken only by the shouts of children scampering across the dirt yards or rushing pell-mell into the narrow street. A series of small lanes and cul-de-sacs lent an air of New Orleans elegance to the district. Some of the pavement stones and brick sidewalks bore elaborate insignias and designs.

We turned up one stone-paved street and parked in front of a huge Victorian house. This particular house had a new coat of paint on the outside and a beautifully restored stained glass window near its entry.

He and I went up the stoop, rang the doorbell, and were immediately greeted by a gangly-looking young man with a gregarious Southern drawl who excitedly invited us in.

Barry Cole was the name of the young man, although everyone called him "B. C." He was from the country but had landed like an orphan on the doorstep of Bill Wright's house. Bill Wright, the man who started the hotline, was just a few paces behind Barry, carrying in his hands several bags of crushed ice. Dark-haired, middle-aged, he looked more like a suburban family man from the Midwest, and he dressed like one, too. Bill struck me as being straight as they come. The only betrayal of his gayness came in the form of rather furtive, lascivious glances occasionally fired about the room at B. C. All in all, Bill projected an air of great stability. A practical man, and a handy one at that, his every move about the house and the kitchen showed a quiet knowingness and strength.

Bill was divorced from his wife in Colorado, who had retained custody of their five-year-old daughter. Bill would fly back every chance he got to sit in a rental car and stare at his daughter from afar. The courts had decided he was unfit to visit her because he was gay. He had recently moved East, taking ownership of a store at the local ski resort. He had struck out like a pioneer, newly liberated from his marriage and angry at the discrimination he had faced.

Shades were drawn on all the front windows. Tape and two boards covered several empty panes, the result of a recent police raid. B. C. grabbed one of the bags of ice from Bill and handed me the other. The two of them led me to the kitchen, where a whole crowd had gathered, eagerly involved in the afternoon's preparations. One man of color, wearing a bright pink polo shirt and tight jeans and with straightened jet-black hair, was the spitting image of the black actor Billy Dee Williams. His name was Ed. I learned that he and B. C. were the best of friends, bonded by their "orphan" status. Both men had been thrown out of their houses and had left the country to pursue careers. B. C. worked around Bill's house and had an on-again, off-again relationship with Bill. Ed was a waiter at a local upscale restaurant who was trying to put together his modeling portfolio. He had recently done an ad in a clothing catalog for a company out of North Carolina and was still reeling from his success.

The chatter for the next half hour revolved around the recent "talent night" that Bill had thrown in the house as an event to raise money for the hotline. A drag show with lip-synching to popular music had attracted a variety of local men to compete. B. C. lost out to a local court judge who did a Mae West number, and he still contended that the contest had been rigged.

The big news of the event involved the police raid that had taken place later that evening. An upstairs bedroom had been converted into a porn theater. A sheet stretched across the window as a movie screen had evidently revealed its sordid images to neighbors below, who had looked away in disbelief. Ostensibly, the police had arrived to charge that alcoholic drinks were being served illegally. Just when it had looked as though arrests were to be made, the judge, divested of his Mae West drag, had come forward and struck a quick deal with the officers. Bill had paid a fine and the charges had been dropped.

For this reason, only soda was being served. Around three o'clock, everyone congregated in the parlor. Bill, B. C., and Ed and their buddies were joined by a large array of men of different ages and different social sets. I was the "new blood" in town, and I felt the close scrutiny of everyone in the room, especially after they heard I had lived in New York City and had been a dancer. B. C. had dreamed of dancing and was mystified how anyone could leave New York City to come back to such a small town.

I enjoyed B. C.; he could cast a tale peopled with local inhabitants I had come to know, transforming them into tragic and comic characterizations of themselves. B. C. referred to Ed as his "black sister," and the two had centered their existence around goading and teasing each other relentlessly.

Another regular at Bill's house was a kid named George who had been a divinity student at Jerry Falwell's school. A red-haired lad with freckles who had spent a year and a half in the dorms of Falwell's college before escaping its claustrophobic social atmosphere, George spoke like an ex-disciple of Sun Myung Moon. There was all the zeal of a born-again gay man in his voice. He pierced his ear, shaved his head, took a room near Bill's back porch, and immediately began manning the phones for the hotline.

At that first afternoon gathering, I also met the other gay men who had settled in the historic district and, like Bill, were renovating houses. The judge showed up a few minutes late, followed by his lover, the doctor. Though they shared a house downtown, I learned they led a life of relative secrecy. The doctor was divorced and kept an apartment, for appearances' sake. He paid his ex-wife well not to talk. Together, they were a mirthful, fun couple, but in a matter of minutes, they could disengage like two complete strangers.

Another couple in the group included a young liberal lawyer who worked for the Civil Liberties Union and his lover, a graphic artist and architectural preservationist. Together the two had managed to turn around two houses. They would fix up a place in twelve months, sell it, and then move on to the next adventure. Their new project was a house located off of Madison Street, the heart of the historic area. It was a huge Federal-style mansion, complete with a ballroom and an aviary.

I also met a male nurse and his lover, a native Hawaiian who did extensive landscaping around their house. "Miss Pineapple" was the unofficial nickname of the Hawaiian, a reference to both his heritage and his habit of walking around his yard wearing a large yellow muumuu. Miss Pineapple was credited with building the huge power-driven waterfall at the side of their house. The house was frequently featured on Garden Week tours.

After an amusing chat with Ed, the waiter, I was cornered in the back kitchen by the ever loquacious B. C., who wanted to gossip and hear my tales of New York. B. C. referred to himself as "Miss Welcome Wagon, herself." Ed referred to B. C. as "Miss Doormat," as he was frequently the victim of impossible love affairs with "men who just walked all over him." This was shown by his affections for both the "chicken hawk," Bill, and an abusive funeral director that he had lived with in his rural township. B. C. spilled the beans on everybody. I learned inside of an hour or more that men with whom I had grown up in the community lived, underground, secret lives that were far different from what I had ever imagined.

My laundromat flame was a familiar trick to the others in the community. Everyone, it turns out, had had him at some time or other. B. C. told me that my friend had had every conceivable form of venereal disease known to mankind. At that moment, I realized that ours was a doomed affair. I was afraid of catching venereal warts or hepatitis or, even worse, the ill-defined new "gay disease" and having to explain it to my father, the doctor. Feelings of jealousy mixed with hypochondria came over me. I couldn't help but obsess on the fact that my date was probably "having" everyone else in town.

The support group talked catalogs and housing outlets. They compared swatches of fabric and shades of color. They talked antiquing and kitchen shopping, all between consoling this and that terribly insecure young thing. I was impressed by both their knowledge and their compassion. The old run-down squalor of the antebellum neighborhood was being given a face-lift, and confused, young lives were being mended. The sheer enthusiasm of the group was infectious.

Much later, I found myself engaged in close conversation with an attractive fellow named Chris, who persuaded me to come see the renovations on his house. I walked to Chris's with my laundromat friend in tow, and we viewed the once-beautiful interiors of a Georgian-style house still in the throws of being restored to its former grandeur. We walked across the half-finished floors of the dining room to emerge in his new kitchen—modern and cooled by a large air-conditioner. A television mounted on the wall was broadcasting the evening news. The kitchen sported marble countertops, drawers filled with expensive cutlery, a butcher-block table, and Euro-style cabinets with sleek lines. It was a fastidious work of art, the first focus of Chris's labor in two years of owning the house. Only the kitchen and two upstairs bedrooms had been completed and modernized; the rest of the house was a mess of dust and scaffolding.

It was love at first sight when Chris showed me the second bedroom on the second floor. Through its window, I could see the Blue Ridge Mountains and the skyline. The room's walls were pale blue, and its fireplace had the original glazed tiles. The floorboards were a rich red tone. A large antique wood four-poster bed and a desk gave it the clean, aesthetic feel of an artist's studio from the nineteenth century. I congratulated Chris on his efforts.

"You need a place to live?" he asked. "I'm looking for a roommate." So it was I found my second home in town. It was only a matter of weeks before I moved from my quiet street in a straight neighborhood to that small Southern gay ghetto that had sprung up invisibly, and seemingly overnight, in the heart of the city.

My room became the one I'd seen on the tour. Chris's bedroom, which was down the hall, was always covered in dust. It was a simple room—one oriental rug, one chair, and a cot for a bed. A rough table made of wood planks served as his desk. Those first summer nights I'd find him lying on his bed fully nude, the door halfway open, an antique globe lamp glowing at a low setting, and his carpenter pants and paint-soiled T-shirt tossed on the floor. In the morning, he dressed in crisply starched dress shirts with ties to go to the department store where he worked as a buyer and design consultant. His dress shoes were always spit-polish clean.

Chris worked on his house every weekend, playing his Hall and Oates or David Bowie cassettes and moving about with paintbrush in hand, body speckled with sweat and dust. Chris's lean arms and the bare sides of his chest that peeked through his painter's overalls shone in the dust sifting about in the evening sunlight.

The first few summer nights after I moved in, we sat in his back-yard, resembling a set from a Tennessee Williams play, surrounded by clapboard siding, listening to the night sounds—train whistles, peepers, and the shouts of kids from the low-income housing down the block. The air was filled with the smell of baking bread, coming from the bakery mill down by the railroad tracks. Chris was working to make new what had become impossibly old and overgrown, and with his help, the hundred-year-old house was reclaiming its former glamour. In the lemon half-light of evening, it stood noble and elegant.

A few nights later, Chris lay back in a wrought-iron lawn chair with huge cushions and began to speak, his voice hanging disembodied in the evening air. I watched his narrow red lips, always chapped, and the movement of his bearded chin as he spoke. I could see the cool lime pulp lingering in his glass when he tipped it to drink. He wore jean cutoffs, without underwear, revealing a long, lanky dick hugging the inside of his leg. He stared contemplatively at the house, his creation, his lifetime project. He commented about this or that new plan, ever mindful of architectural styles. He described the sundeck and the small glassed-in porch that would come off the back. Then we talked about my boyhood in the town and how it was back then. I shared with him memories of driving by this very same neighborhood with my father, seeing its boarded-up houses and decrepit porches and thinking how the whole place would be torn down in a matter of years. It was once just one more reason to flee what I viewed as a dying, neglected southern way of life. And I told him about my loneliness and my late-in-life sexual awakening.

Chris described his own boyhood and coming-of-age in California. "I lost my cherry when I was fifteen to a California State Trooper. He picked me up in his convertible and took me home to his apartment. He was a nice man. I was young, scared, but he was very understanding. I thought I was in love."

"Did you see him again?"

"Oh, a couple of times. He lived in Laguna Hills. He'd take me to his place and give me a beer. It was only once or twice."

"It seems like a fantasy."

"It was."

"When did you go to 'Nam?" I asked Chris, having heard about his tour of duty from the lesbian couple down the street.

"I left when I was seventeen. I signed up. My father was a career officer. I wanted to go. It was really what I was expected to do, and I didn't give it another thought."

He took a sip of his gin and tonic. The sky was growing darker.

"Do you regret going?"

"I didn't know any better. I was so young."

"What was it like?" All I could think of were the old World War II movies I had seen on TV and then the war photos in *Time* magazine—newscasters, soldiers, exotic stills of temples, Buddhist monks on fire.

"Saigon was beautiful. I did my first tour there. I worked in the intelligence office. It was a large complex outside of the main city—bunker huts connected by passages and tunnels—barbed wire. I stayed in a beautiful French-style hotel in the old part of the town. I had a mamasan."

"Was that unusual?"

"No. It was so cheap. There was no reason not to. This old woman would get up and make the coffee and prepare a breakfast. She washed my clothes. She lived with me the entire year and then some. She had a grandchild that she went home to see on the weekends. I never found out what happened to her. I left before the Tet Offensive."

I took a sip of my drink. We were quiet. The night air was still and beautiful. I could smell the roses Chris had pruned and watered during the day.

"Every morning they sent a car to pick me up and take me to work. It was very routine. I saw very little that was actual war or combat. In late day I could go out on my own through the city. I would walk along the riverfront and the wharfs."

"The city's on a river?"

"Yeah, floating houseboats and restaurants. The lights at night were really lovely. I loved walking through the city, just walking for hours. I was never fearful. I would wander into the temples." He paused. "I became a Buddhist."

"You did?"

"I found peace of mind in the religion. It was very much a part of the culture. You almost had to embrace it if you spent any time there. I thought nothing strange about it. There was another American who taught me. He spoke some of the language. When it was time to come back here I signed on for a second tour."

"Why did you want to go back again?"

"Again, I didn't think much about it. I had nothing to come back to in the States. I was very much into honor and country. "

"What made you finally leave?"

The evening was turning damp. The moon was beginning to rise. No lights were on in the house. He shifted in his chair.

"Me and this other guy started having sex. We got close. They found out. He turned me in. I was discharged for being gay. My father lobbied to get it changed to an honorable discharge. He succeeded. They spared me the court-martial. It was a long protracted affair. It was a bad time, a very bad time."

Chris stood up and moved to the edge of the yard with his drink.

"And I sort of went mad . . . I mean, dropped out, for a long time. I didn't know who I was."

We both remained silent. Then, he turned the subject back to Virginia, his job, and the neighbors. He told me more stories about Miss Pineapple, about Donnie and Rick, the gay hairdressers, notorious in town for their S&M leather parties. But then he stopped, stifled a yawn, and stood to say good night. At the top of the stairs, he gave me one long, wistful look. An attraction was definitely forming between us.

Every night after that I thought about him. I dreamed about his solitary figure walking beside the boats and lights of an aging Saigon. I thought about a handsome young teen in a car being fondled by a cop with sunglasses. I thought of the silence of the house and the way he had ended up here, far from California and far from the war, and I wondered if he would find someone to live with him in the house. He told me it was his dream to settle down.

I began to listen for his door opening in the late night, for the sound of him in the hall, and I thought of his body and the way he wore his jeans. He didn't seem afraid of anything. I watched the way he worked about the house. He didn't hold back. I held back everything, and I tried to imagine myself going off to war and doing all he had done, owning a house in a strange southern town, starting a new life. And yet a new life had started for me. My life seemed less about my studies or returning back North, and more about building a home with Chris.

I couldn't imagine what my parents would make of this. They probably thought of me as collapsed over my books and counting the minutes until my departure. When I first told them of my decision to move to Madison Street, they had looked at me in horror. Madison Street was the place for junkies, welfare recipients, desperate liber-als, not a doctor's son, but they said nothing and accepted it as further proof of my troubled state of mind. As long as I continued in my stud-ies at school and made good grades, they were happy. Unlike my pre-vious existence, I was now becoming a part of a clique of gay men who were teaching me something about being young again. I had let go of some of my city pretensions and begun to accept the newer cus-toms of the Southern gay ghetto. House renovating; private black-tie dinner parties; assignations at the mall; trips to The Park, an after-hours gay and lesbian disco—these were the rituals of my new world.

The Park was a place of wild dancing. Gay men and lesbians who had to go about their lives in close invisibility unleashed the pent-up energies of a whole week. A number of voyeurs, local straights, came to look and be seen and to indulge in the "decadence." The Park was also the place for catching up and sharing within the community, such as it was. Unlike New York, where I had wandered Christopher and the Upper West Side anonymously, barely ever spoken to in the dark bars, and sometimes dismissed with one look at my manner of dress, at The Park I felt immediately welcome. In truth, the discos of New York, where a velvet rope frequently kept one waiting in the cold for hours, held no allure for me anymore. At The Park, however, I was a big fish in a small pond, reveling in the bizarre mix of people, some freakier than any I had met in New York.

Chris was just another odd and special friend I found flourishing in this pond, washed up by life's troubles to this quiet Virginia backwater. Working side by side with him on the house, I began to grow in my appreciation and love for the neighborhood and its history. I loved his obsession with fine antiques, the way decoration and hospitality came first and offset all other goals and aspirations. Life seemed so simple with this one focus in mind. It was as though Chris intended to wipe away any trace of his difficult past.

I was in the hallway of the judge's house when I first kissed Chris. It was after a dinner to which I was invited through Chris's intervention. Over the months I had become more and more attracted to him. We had studied each other for days. After wine and drinks we drove back to the house.

It was odd entering the house, the huge downstairs unfinished and dark. Once upstairs he pulled me into his bedroom. His skin and body were different close up from what I had expected. He was covered with scratches, coarse almost, plain. He was muscular, but without a soft or youthful look. It was an older body, strong, but worn. It was not sensual. There was something hardened about it. His touch was without emotion. He was enormously endowed, and that alone was a turn-on, but he never seemed to grow fully hard. His mouth was all over me, without restraint; he licked my body everywhere.

He made me come quickly, while his own orgasm was labored and difficult, almost violent. He preferred bringing himself off, slapping, beating, tugging at himself with a ferocity that went beyond simple pleasure.

When it was over, I sat on the edge of his bed. He pulled on his pants and went to the bathroom. When he returned, he was calm, as though nothing had happened. As I dressed, I realized the odd proximity of our rooms. I was two doors down the hall. I was in his house. Did this mean we were lovers? Should I stay in his bedroom?

"Good night," he said.

"Good night," I replied.

I did not see him for three days. On the weekend, I came home to find him painting again. He smiled. "Oh, hi. How was your week?"

"Long."

I had been studying for a chemistry final. I was trying to get into a program to be a physical therapist. I had given myself a year to finish the prerequisites.

He smiled. "You want a beer? I'll cook us a steak on the grill."

I nodded my head in appreciation. I wondered if we'd talk about our sexual encounter from the other night, but he seemed to have forgotten it.

An hour later we were in the backyard. He had marinated the steaks; they were on the grill. It was a cool fall evening. The stars had appeared. He loaded up the plates with food. He pulled some beers from the fridge. I felt terribly young beside him, even though I knew he was only five years older. I thought of his time and experience in Vietnam.

After finishing a piece of steak, he started to explain. "I lived in the hills of Colorado, just above Denver, after I got back. I don't know why I ended up in Denver. I can't remember half of those times. Once a week I came down into town. I stood in this park and hustled. The cars would pull up—business men, married men. They would proposition; I would turn tricks. I did everything imaginable. I was out-of-my-head crazy. The shack I lived in was condemned. No one knew I lived there. There was no running water. I was out of it, but I went on like that for three years."

I remained quiet and finished my piece of steak. There was no emotion or remorse in his voice. He spoke in a factual way, as though recounting the story of a stranger's life.

"After a while I had enough. I decided to come East. I found a job in a local store doing their window displays. After a while I became so good at it, they hired me to do other work. So I came here with the store. My dad has relocated to Richmond."

"Your dad who's in the service?"

"Yeah. He remarried. My mother died. He and my stepmother and I don't speak anymore."

"So you plan on staying here?"

"Yeah, I love it here. It's where I want to be. In a year or two, the house will be finished. Maybe I'll sell it and start another; maybe I won't. My needs are really small."

I tried to imagine the two of us living in the house. I tried to imagine staying in the town with him and entering his world, making a new life from something old on that old street, maybe taking up writing or painting and remaining a native son in the town.

"It's strange for me to have grown up here and to have wanted nothing better than to get away and to now have reason to stay," I replied.

He looked at me with a grin and laughed. "Finish your steak."

Late that night I lay in my bed thinking. We turned in without a kiss. I was alone in my bedroom. I wanted to go to him. An hour went by. I tried reading. I put the book down. I was thinking about the idea of staying. Could I live with him? Could I just quit the idea of returning to New York and settle down? I must have brooded for an hour in the dark of my room. I could see the moonlight on the yard and the mountainsides. Summer was gone. Fall had arrived. The outdoor heating oil tanks would soon be filled to heat the three-story welfare houses, and holiday decorations would be taped to their plastic-covered windows.

I walked down the hall to his door. It was shut. I knocked. I knocked again. It was unlocked. I went in. He was awake. I was going to tell him about staying.

"Hi."

"Hi," he replied in the dark of the room.

"I thought maybe I could sleep with you," I said uneasily, my voice carrying with it all the urgency and seriousness of a life-shattering proposal.

"I just jacked off. If I'd only known earlier, I would have waited for you—sorry."

I paused, uncomfortable, feeling foolish. "Yeah, well." I was quiet. I still wanted just to lie there with him, to hear him speak, but I didn't know how to convey it.

"I'm pretty tired," he said.

I did not know whether to tell him that I just wanted to hold him, that I was going to ditch my plans for school, that I wanted to sit at his desk and write all day, to help him finish the house. I waited. I wanted him to make some move, but he didn't. My hesitation didn't surprise him. He seemed used to late-night intruders, especially those half-clothed and confused. A moment later he was snoring. I got up and went out the door, and that was it; my life fate seemed sealed, my choice to be with him dashed.

He was out a lot the following week. That weekend I helped him about the house, but I could never find the courage to approach him. He showed no sign one way or the other. He never spoke of us with any intimacy. Something had changed between us, or maybe he was protecting me, trying not to sway me from a future he thought I really wanted. I thought that he probably saw me as too mixed up, too insecure, too indirect about my wants and needs.

A month later, I came home with a sore throat and fever. All day, I had been sweating and chill. I climbed into bed and turned off the light. Chris came into the room, without a word. The next thing I knew, we were having sex. Chris was aggressive, rough. I lay passive, unmoving. He seemed to want the pleasure to be all mine. He was at my waist, pulling my damp sweatpants from my body. He was at my thighs and all over me, with a hungry tongue and lips.

No sooner had it ended than he left. A terrible silence descended on the house. We were each in our separate bedrooms, just a few doors away, but more than isolated. I could almost hear his thoughts. He probably could hear mine.

The next day, while he was out, I entered his bedroom. I studied the carpet, the cot, the desk. I was so desirous to reach him, to break through. I began to think I was too passive an individual for him. He was so self-sufficient, and I was not.

Then spring came with amazing beauty, especially around the time of the Garden Tour, when local residents put their homes on display and yards and terraces overflowed with wisteria. The lesbians' house was open and on view. I had applied to several universities, despite my half-hearted intent to remain near Chris.

I did not want to go back to New York. It was my intention to go further south to Duke University or to move to Richmond, but when the acceptance from Columbia arrived, it was hard to pass up. My father had gone there in his younger days, and so I elected to carry on the tradition, to return to New York, still fearful of the growing news of the gay plague that had descended upon Manhattan.

The next month I began packing to leave. It was an exquisitely sunny day at the end of my second summer on Madison Street, and the end of my second year in the town. Chris was raking grass cuttings. B. C. had come over to help him. I had my train ticket to New York in my pocket.

Chris continued raking, but then he looked up and smiled. "You need help?"

"I'll manage."

He came over to the car. I looked back at the house. It was yellow in the afternoon light, beautiful, with its graceful walls and trim lawn. The shades in the old house were drawn up. A man was cleaning the windows.

"Look, someone is finally working next door. It's about time."

"Yeah," I grinned. "Well, thanks. I'll miss things here. "

"Yeah. Come visit," B. C. hollered.

"You too."

I was sad to leave. The neighborhood looked as sleepy and lively as it ever had, the two extremes coexisting. The civil liberties lawyer was painting his porch. Bill was carrying some groceries in for the next social. I drove away and never looked back.

Sometimes late at night, I think about Chris's house on Madison Street and remember myself feeling alone in that upstairs bedroom, contemplating my decision to leave. In retrospect, I could not have stayed. Too close to home and my childhood, I would have remained that passive boy, always on the edge of conversation, always on the edge of desire.

Chris died of AIDS two years after I left. Something in him seemed doomed from the start, and I was not surprised. It was as though the war, sooner or later, would catch up with him. I would have been helpless to have saved him. He was shut down inside; there was one part of him I never could have reached.

The house is still there. I've since passed by, admiring its bright yellow siding and white trim. Someone else took possession of it and treated it with obvious devotion, although this past Easter I noticed a "For Sale" sign hovering on its front lawn. I guess the street itself has still not totally turned around, its past still too tarnished and abject to win full favor and approval.

– 11 –

Revelation

Thomas L. Long

While Monsignor Abbot muses upon the insouciance of Negroes and smells the inside of his nostrils by pinching them slightly, inhaling in quick sniffs, he feels his heart clench its last beats. An exquisite pain pulses up his side, hot and sharp, like the spasm of a long-deferred ejaculation. An unfiltered Chesterfield cigarette drops from his hand onto the edge of the coffee saucer, and his face, which has assumed a look of astonishment, falls into the plate of half-eaten eggs, runny side up, about whose undercooked consistency he has just chastised Calvina Luther, thus ensuring that she will not check on him for a very long time, allowing the dainty pollen of pine trees and dogwoods, blown through open windows on the May breeze, to settle on his white shirt's French cuffs. The cufflinks are sterling silver: a lamb with victory banner, the Latin motto *Bonus pastor.*

Awaiting discovery in monsignor's suite above the dining room is a locked fireproof filing cabinet, which he has told Calvina and the parish secretary, Miss Edna, holds his archives of annulment cases from the marriage tribunal. In fact, they are meticulous files of young men, mostly guests in the rectory (where candidates for seminary stay while they undergo the archdiocese's rigorous battery of psychological and personality tests, and seminarians visit because monsignor's hospitality is legendary: generous home cooking and a well-stocked bar, the only stipulation being that one can drink as much as one likes provided that one uses the shot glass to measure). Each accordion folder contains the following: one or more color photographs of the young man (monsignor always has just a few more exposures

left in his camera that he wants to use up); stained underpants in a
sealed plastic freezer bag with the young man's name, approximate
age, and date of visit written in the white spaces on the bag; a three-
by-five note card on which are taped pubic hairs retrieved from the
guest room toilet where the young man has stayed; a form on which
monsignor has made punctilious notes on the young man and on his own
masturbatory fantasies while inhaling the file's redolent contents.
Each young man afterward notices that he is missing underpants, but
young men do not discuss that kind of intelligence with one another,
thus missing the opportunity to comprehend one of the larger patterns
in their sacred cosmos.

   While Calvina Luther contemplates the apocalypse of white folks,
she slams pots, pans, the dishwasher racks and door, and cupboards
loud enough to raise the dead. Her freckled, honey skin has assumed
the darker shades (her pressure's up) that her husband and children
call "The Wrath That Is to Come." She has cooked and cleaned for
these unmarried Catholic men for two decades and remains as mystified today about their powers over the divine and the demonic and
about their ways. She loves them in the way you'd love a dog with
three legs or an idiot child. Some of their eccentricity she attributes to
whiteness—the priest who changed his undershorts three times a day
and insisted that they be laundered daily, the priest who never left his
room except for meals or morning mass, the priest who never let her
enter his suite but left his towels and bed linens neatly outside his
locked door—all consistent with what her mother and grandmother
had told her: They smells bad, they dirty, they like roaches you never
can get rid of. However, Calvina is of a new generation, believing that
white folks, unlike the poor, thou shalt not always have with you.
   In the dining room, Monsignor Abbot's lips have turned a deep
purple and his face a slate blue. His bowels and bladder have evacu-
ated their contents into his silk boxer shorts, and his eyes have taken
the cloudy gelatinous hue of a fish's on ice. The Chesterfield cigarette
has burned nearly to the end, and the butt is now poised on the edge of
the saucer. In the locked closet of his bedroom above hang leather and
metal appurtenances: cowhide studded vest and armbands, harnesses,
stainless steel cock rings, and other erotic technologies belonging to a

man known only as "Monk," the addressee of numerous letters to a post office box in a suburb of Rome, North Carolina. In the weeks to follow there will accumulate piles of dead letters, greeting, "Dear Monk, I sure had a good time with you when you came here last month. I loved the way you stuck your fingers up my ass while chewin' on my tits and jerkin' me off"; "Dear Monk, you can always cum back to this bitch; he's got a hole for you to plug. You pull your big rig right up to this trailer, whore, and ride me all up and down the highway"; "Monk, how come you don't call no more, did I do something wrong?"; " Monk, I been a bad boy, whorin' all over the county, and need my daddy to put me over his knee to give me a good whuppin'." Monk's nipples are pierced, sometimes decorated by custom-made gold pins, Greek letters, alpha in the right nipple, omega in the left. He only wears them when he visits his pen pals.

Calvina goes to her tool drawer (top drawer of the last cabinet by the outside door—string, old bread bags, plastic bag ties, rumpled foil, scissors, rounded worn flat-head screwdriver, rubber bands with newspaper ink smudges, worn copy of Fatima's *Dream Book,* BC Powder envelopes) and takes out a pack of Newport cigarettes, lighting one with the flame of the stove. Monsignor has forbidden her to smoke in the kitchen, telling her it is vulgar and unsanitary. But he has riled her enough today, and his own cigarettes as he lingers over coffees, she thinks, will mask hers. She takes a Royal Crown Cola bottle out of the refrigerator and pops it open; sliding a drinking straw into the bottle, she alternates sips and cigarette puffs.

Monsignor's Chesterfield cigarette has dropped to the tablecloth, where its ember begins to make a relentlessly expanding epiphany. He has accommodated Miss Edna's thrift and Calvina's flagging energies by permitting a cotton/polyester permanent press cloth on weekdays, though he insists on linen damask for Sunday meals. The cigarette burns an aureole on the cloth, which suddenly flames into fanning wings like those of seraphs. Soon the cloth is a holocaust, kindling his clothes and the table.

Thinking better of smoking in the kitchen and still stinging from Monsignor's scolding about the eggs, Calvina pushes herself up from the kitchen chair, adjusts the blue bandanna around her hair, before stepping into the breezeway outside the kitchen. She finds Pegram by the trash cans; the parish's janitor is cleaning tools with a solvent that,

as it wafts past her cigarette, makes her think of church barbecues. She
adjusts her bandanna again and straightens the bodice of her uniform
with one hand while smoking with the other.

"Fine day, Miz Calvina," Pegram says.

"Fine enough," she replies.

"I gotta be careful with this cleaner, work with it out in the air, keep
it away from fire," he says.

"Uh hm." She is thinking about mens, the new hat she will wear to
church—purple felt, a blossom of tulle, a peacock's feather—and
wondering, for the sixty-seventh time this year, what would ever
make a grown man give up women to become a priest. Mmh-mmh-
mmh. She shrugs, shakes her head, and concludes that her mother and
grandmother were right about white people. Pegram has finished his
task and throws the soaked rags into the trash can.

"Pegram," she says, "Monsignor was complainin' about the blinds
in the parish office. You seen to them yet?"

"I'll get to it by-an'-by," he says, looking cross.

"I'm not tellin' you your bidness, mind you, but I just got such a
tongue lashin' 'bout my eggs. Word to the wise," she explains.

"What about your eggs?"

"Too eggy, I s'pose."

Pegram laughs and walks away shaking his head, while Calvina
takes one more drag of the cigarette and drops it in the trash can. She
walks to a fringe of dirt beside the parking lot behind the rectory
where she has planted violets, squats down, and begins to pull weeds.

Many of Monk's pen pals have finished high school. Some of them
live with their parents, or with cousins, or with a girlfriend, and one with
a wife and child. They meet Monk in the parking lots of motels off the
interstate highway; he gives them a hundred dollars cash to register with
the manager and never asks them for the change afterward. If they ever
wonder who this man is in black socks and dress shoes, leather cap, vest,
and harnesses, they never ask. Even while he calls them names—"You
nigger lovin' cock suckin' piece of white trash shit"—there is a kind of
aloof gentility in his voice, like that of a TV talk show host or an under-
taker. He never kisses them, but after the scene is consummated, he allows their heads to rest on his chest while they both smoke, and he

strokes their hair, like a hunter caressing his hounds. He smells of tobacco and Old Spice; they of hair gel and Polo. If they fall asleep, they awake to find Monk has gone. The first time that happens, Monk's pen pal goes to the motel room door and looks out; seeing only his own Camaro, he wonders if he didn't just dream it all, then wonders how a man can just disappear in the twinkling of an eye, like The Rapture.

Calvina has cleared the violet bed of weeds and grunts as she rises to walk back to the rectory kitchen. Smoke snakes from under the trash can lid where she has thrown her cigarette. "Oh My Laws," she says and trots over to the can, lifting the lid, but dropping it instantly when the heat sears her fingers and flames lick out. "Oh My Laws! Oh My Laws!" she shouts. "Pegram, fire!" She runs to the spigot and hose under the breezeway, rolls its length to the trash can, and opens the nozzle, attempting to juggle the hose and the lid without burning herself.

Pegram finds her with flames and water shooting in opposite directions, grabs the hose, and barks at her, "Go tell Miss Edna to call the fire department," which she does by running through the alley between the rectory and the church. He jets water into the can's flames.

Shortly, a single fire engine lumbers around the corner and drives into the parking lot where Pegram has successfully extinguished the trash can. "Everything's under control here," he reassures the firemen, who nonetheless examine the evidence and ask what happened. They are joined by Calvina, who gives her own account (without the cigarette). The initial excitement over, versions of the accident recounted, everyone postpones returning to their stations and to their quotidian dullness. They stand quietly looking at the ground.

On the other side of the rectory, the dining room is clothed with the sun: draperies and wallpaper burn like sins purged from penitent souls, coiling and writhing around the greasy form that used to be Monsignor Abbot, his flesh tanned to black hide. Its doors closed, the room has become a bubble that suddenly breaks through the morning with a booming roar as the window glass explodes.

"What in hell?!" the fire chief shouts, as his crew runs to the side of the rectory, where they find flames and smoke rising up to the second story and singeing the resinous branches of the pines. Like an army frantic in the ultimate battle, the firemen start to work, call in a second and a third alarm, and try to protect the brick church, if the frame rectory cannot be saved. Then the steady roar of the fire is broken by a falling crash that shakes the ground like heavenly spheres collapsing into ān infinite abyss: the second floor, including Monsignor Abbot's filing cabinet, has dropped to the ground. Calvina sobs inconsolably, not yet aware that she did not cause this fire.

Three days later when the wet charcoal has cooled, the auxiliary bishop of the archdiocese, Fenton Doyle, will fastidiously pick his way through the wreckage with a locksmith to retrieve Monsignor's annulment case files. He is a small, pious man with delicate hands and feet; he will wear floral gardening gloves and rubbers covering his dress shoes, his pectoral cross neatly placed in his shirt pocket. The heat of the fire and the drenching fire hoses will have complicated the locksmith's work (punctuated repeatedly with breathy curses), which will take half an hour, during which Fenton Doyle will finger the beads of the rosary (a gift from his mother on her deathbed as he administered the Last Rites) in his right coat pocket, praying for the soul of his fellow priest. "Sonna bitch!—Sorry, padre." The locksmith will finally open the cabinet. Fenton Doyle will open a middle drawer at his waist level and begin to examine the files, pulling one folder at random, then a second, then a third. He will become very pale and his hands will shake returning each folder. Then he will try another drawer.

He will close the drawers and reset the lock and never speak about it.

– 12 –

Are You the Guy I Used to Know?

Dayton Estes

I returned from my year of postgraduate study in Tuebingen, Germany, and loafed for several months because I couldn't find a job. Not working didn't sit well with my parents. Since my father was on the road most of the week, taking orders for his fertilizer business, I got flak from him only on the weekends. My mother, however, who was an alcoholic in an advanced stage of the disease, was there twenty-four dreadful hours each day, and I ran the risk of being subjected to her continual nagging, suspicion, accusation (much of it true), sometimes physical violence, but always embarrassment if any neighbor or friend of mine visited.

During that uncomfortable year, I took whatever temporary jobs were available and continued to look for a permanent position, but it seemed that either I was too educated or else I was not educated enough, even to fill the job of office boy. So I got a job measuring tobacco acreage at the beginning of the summer.

A German girl I used to hang with in Tuebingen showed up for two weeks on her way back home to Germany. My parents were not only inhospitable and uncivil toward her, but downright mean, fearing that their son would either marry a foreigner, at the worst, or, at least, was up to no good "alone upstairs with that girl."

One day after she left to return to Germany, I caught a ride to Virginia Beach with a person I had met and seen only a few times while in college. He was gay. Though I had previously had a couple of same-sex experiences and had enjoyed them, I would not then have categorized myself as being gay. During the weekend at the beach, however, still harboring the bad taste in my mouth from the friction I endured at home, as well as from my parents' behavior toward Brigitte, I managed to secure a job as a bartender at a gay bar, by chance, not by intention. During the day, my job was to act as bartender, and at night I served as a waiter. Laws relaxing the sale of hard liquor had not yet been realized in most of the South, so bartending meant, for the most part, serving beer, mixing champagne cocktails, and trying to keep the patrons from becoming too drunk and rowdy, for fear that the cops would sniff trouble and use that as a pretext to raid the bar.

I had a ball during the rest of that all too short summer. I did not drink on the job, but I socialized a lot while tending bar. Otherwise, I just kept to myself, constantly fearing that people would ask where I worked. I was always embarrassed to answer honestly, yet glad to be there, glad to have a job. I did manage to pick up a dose of crab lice that summer.

I was very chaste, as well as chased, in those—my younger and more handsome—days, and, too, I was just beginning to enjoy my new mental freedom in the gay life, which seemed to me to approach somewhat the social and intellectual freedom that I had enjoyed as a student and had left behind in Europe. It was only later that the "freedom" of the gay life proved in several ways to be an illusionary hope, but at the time, the gay life offered me more freedom than I had ever known growing up in the United States as a teen, or during my four years in college.

It was the summer of 1960, and the souring of relations with Cuba and the beginnings of the Civil Rights Movement were paramount in everyone's mind. The top was also about to blow off a society too long overdue for change. People were suddenly less afraid to be different, as the dangers of the Cuban Missile Crisis intensified. Fears of a possible atomic war being fought on American soil contributed to and evolved into "love-ins," penetrating deeply and painfully a society repressed in a puritanical and moral straightjacket. Pot was grown, or was at least rampantly available, in almost every town. Other drugs were only just beginning to show up, now and then, at least down South, but alcohol was practically free for the asking, or very cheap.

It was the time when the birth control pill was being made available and beginning to emancipate women, allowing them to enjoy sex without the punishment of an unwanted pregnancy. The pill also proved to be an escape hatch for both men and women, freeing all from the prison of their inhibited sexual lives and repressed fantasies. Soon, it likewise affected gays, in these early days of "free love." The television series *Father Knows Best* epitomized the very structure, or stricture, of middle American society. Adultery was, of course, hush-hush, but widespread. Divorce was known on the soaps but didn't exist among the people "you" knew and was seldom discussed above a whisper. Otherwise, people were not comfortable in admitting the existence of, much less talking about, deviant behavior, such as living with a partner—of either sex—masturbation, homosexuality, alcoholism, drug abuse, even mental illness. As a result of the social pioneers of the 1960s, however, we have a freedom today that was unknown for thousands of years, probably more freedom now than at any time in the history of the world, certainly, though, in the annals of the United States. And it was a happy time for me—that summer of 1960—except that, unbeknownst to me, the "sins" of my fathers were approaching fulfillment, according to the Second Commandment:

. . . for I the Lord thy God am a jealous God and visit the sins of the fathers upon the children unto the third and fourth generation of them that hate me.

I couldn't sleep at night. I would drink whatever beer I took with me back to the room, swill any cheap bourbon I could buy or come by, and spend the rest of the night sleepless, with a sour stomach, waiting for 7 a.m. to come around, when I would go to the grill across the street from my hotel to get a couple of beers and, just incidentally, breakfast. I generally left the breakfast standing and drank whatever they would serve me of beer, or what I could tip the waitress for, return to my cheap room in the attic of the old wooden-frame hotel, which had seen better days, and close my eyes until noon, when I was scheduled to go to work. I seldom enjoyed the luxury of sleep, for some fear or metaphysically inspired guilt was my constant companion, as is the case for many Southern boys.

The "old hotel" consisted, in reality, of only one remaining wing of a much more elaborate resort hotel, which had seen its heyday in the early part of the twentieth century. The rest of the majestic structure had been destroyed by a fire. It still sat, if no longer regally, at least conveniently, on the boardwalk, the center of activity at Virginia Beach, day or night. Guys were always trying to pick up girls in the daytime and early evening. Later on, people went out for exercise; some stepped out for a "fag" (cigarette), some to "commune" with nature, some to enjoy nature in the raw—it was a general meeting place for straights to commiserate with one another about the broads they "just missed out on," or for fairies to meet their types or to pick up a trick, and for people like me, tonight, who for one reason or another couldn't sleep. And I couldn't sleep.

Anyway, this one night, about 2 a.m., my stomach was really churning, and I decided to walk for a while on the boardwalk. I guess I was really lonely. Most people would probably assume that I was "horny," but this was never really an issue with me. I had ways to satisfy that need. In the loneliness of my youth, I had devised other solo delights. (And the loneliness alcoholics and drug addicts experience is particularly frequent and painful.)

Well, this night in question, I had no more beer and my stomach was doing flips and somersaults and couldn't take anymore of the cheap bourbon I had stashed away in my lower drawer. If I walked for a while, I thought, maybe I could get sleepy enough to rest, and the awful headache, that parasitic companion of my loneliness, was threatening to embrace me at any minute. If I could just shut my eyes and drift off for just a moment, perhaps I could get rid of the oncoming headache, or maybe even forget my sour stomach for just a few minutes.

Thus I appeared on the boardwalk about 2 a.m., standing in the shadows of a couple parked cars, watching as the stragglers, rejects of the day, passed listlessly by in the well-lit promenade area. No girls dared be seen out so late, as you would see today, sometimes a couple — boy and a girl—now and then a guy, but nothing to attract the attention of this connoisseur of masculine beauty, and God had not yet granted me the gift to appreciate fully that His delicate workmanship is not limited to the outward and visible.

"Hullo! Wow! What a guy!" Dirty-blond, rather curly hair, handsome, though not tan, slim, 5'10" or 11", white Levis, and *cute*. He had on a blue sport shirt that enhanced his arms, which had just enough hair not to be noticeable (I imagined, even from a distance), and he was passing by the area where I was standing in the shadows, observing, watching his supple movements, his casual gait. "What the hell was he doing out here this late?" God had also not yet granted me the confidence to rely on His "coincidences."

Two men, looking to be in their midthirties and nondescript, had apparently been following him for a while, gradually catching up to him, and one was trying to engage him in conversation. He obviously did not want their attention or company, for he seemed quite ill at ease and kept making attempts as if to break away, but each time, one of the men would extend a tentacle of conversation and again try to seize his prey. The boy was apparently too naive to realize what they wanted or too polite to tell them to buzz off. I heard the ultimate line for starting a conversation—"Got a cigarette?" And I saw him fumble in his shirt pocket and reach out a pack to one of the men. The next question in this stepping-stones process to making a pickup was—"Got a match?"

I don't know what made me do it, perhaps the liquor, maybe the headache, concomitant to the loneliness that had by now attacked me full force. Maybe I was indeed horny. I don't know. At any rate, I stepped out of my observation post in the shadows, walked up to the three, stopped, and said to the blond kid, "Hey, John, these two guys trying to pick you up? Come on, kid, let's go. I told you this morning I would be a little late." The blond "kid" astutely took the hint, seized the opportunity to escape, pretending he knew me. The two losers were left standing, yet they couldn't say anything without betraying their intentions. So they started bickering with each other as we walked off. As it turned out, we really did know each other from some years before, though we didn't realize it immediately.

An odd expression on his face, he suddenly asked, "Are you the guy I used to know down in Chapel Hill? I believe you played the piano at the Canterbury Club, and very well, too." It turned out I was the guy, but that bit about playing the piano very well was just a compliment on his part. It turned out that he had also graduated from Chapel Hill, had done some teaching, and had earned a master's degree in music. He had been promised a good job in the Norfolk school system. I, in turn, told him how I had been in the army and in Germany on a Fulbright Scholarship. I was several years older. I had indeed banged the piano for the Canterbury group for a couple of years, until he entered as a freshman. He was a much better pianist, so I yielded to him, but then I graduated, and that was the last I had seen of him in over six years. We had never really gotten to know each other and were just speaking acquaintances during that one year in Chapel Hill.

"If you don't have anywhere to go or anything to do," I said, not knowing what I was getting myself into, "we can go up to my hotel room for a while, have a drink, and you can stay there, if you wish, and go back home in the morning." Alcoholics, even those beginning their *cursus potum,* always have faith that somewhere, somehow they will be able to get a drink, for, after all, God watches over us alcoholics. I think all alcoholics cynically console themselves with this thought, or perhaps I should say *desperately console themselves,* for we drink alcohol like it is going out of style, or better, for us, any alcohol at all is like Maxwell House coffee, "good to the last drop." Gays, on the other hand, often have a different agenda. Save a shot for anyone you might luck into, and that could prove to be your ticket to a good lay. And at my stage, the cunning nature of the incipient gay mind had powerfully justified the beginning to a baffling addiction.

"Nah, I have to get back home to Norfolk, have to get up tomorrow, but if you don't mind, I'll come stay for a while and have that drink."

We then hurried to my room in the rundown hotel, passing a suspicious desk clerk, who also instinctively knew he would later be requited if he pretended to be dozing. I was perhaps a novice but not totally inept in dealing with addiction, or with a lifestyle or behavior that at that time was still illegal, even punishable by a five- to twenty-year sentence if the perpetrator should end up in court, be tried, and get convicted.

Bunky, that was the blond kid's real name, or rather the nickname I had known him by when we were in college, eventually explained that he really needed to take me up on my invitation to stay for a while because he had drunk too much to drive even the short stretch back to Norfolk. We got to the room, skipped the cheap bourbon I had hoarded, and lay down on the iron bed the hotel provided the summer beach help. Although very little was said, we communicated volumes to each other. In looking back, I think Bunky was headed for trouble in his life, if that night was any indication of things to come, but I was definitely on the road to alcoholism and also headed for problems in my emotional life, neither of which could I foresee.

I held him tight, but he was very tense. He lay there, mentally resisting my every move. Yet he made no effort to leave. I cuddled and kissed him all over, ran my fingers playfully through his beautiful curly blond hair. I rubbed and kissed his hairless abdomen, delicately nibbled on each hard nipple, ran my hand up and down his muscular thighs, cupped his scrotum. The instant I began to ease back his foreskin, he suddenly stopped the struggle within himself and surrendered.

For a time we became one, but there was no time; none existed in this act of faith, just the trust and desire of the person for the moment, an interval that could never take place again for me, and I have a feeling that for him, there has been no repeat. We didn't whisper secrets of the past to each other, nor hopes for the future; there was nothing to confide. We didn't feign a love; we confessed a loneliness and a hunger for each other. We were both locked into a track—he, destined for marriage but starved for male companionship, for a friend he could trust and love, even if only for tonight. I would do graduate study, and marriage was likewise in the cards for me, six years down the road. But I was also starved for someone to love, as well as for his body. And for just a few moments, we rashly crossed over into eternity, and it was indescribably beautiful. Tomorrow would be another day, and the sun would either ease the pain of our temporary love or cleanse us from the guilt forever.

In the 1960s, there were no gay ghettos, no open gay society such as exists now. No professional person would ever have dared confess to being gay. A gay bar, like where I worked, was a den of lowlifes where you went to escape the straightjacket of middle-class society, and where you could *live and breathe freedom* for just a few precious minutes. You could get syphilis or clap or the crabs, maybe even get mugged or knifed, but absolutely the worst risk you took by frequenting a gay bar was a police raid. The cops could, and would, arrest you merely on the suspicion of being homosexual, and God help you if you were ever caught in the act. The newspapers, those guardians of public morality and legal voyeurs, smugly saw to it that you were ruined and your family humiliated. Many good people committed suicide because they had been cited in newspaper accounts of police raids as being suspected of "inverted behavior" or of being perverts. During these years, I had at least four friends who were driven to violence against themselves. Two of these boys I liked very much; the other two had been very close friends. Three of the best college professors and scholars I have ever known were "recognized" for their "accomplishments" and were consequently fired. The Jesuits got one hell of a postulant; Sweden got the other as a citizen. The third, a renowned scholar, brother of an FBI agent, was one day granted a sabbatical by the university and simply "slipped" in the bathtub and broke his neck.

Bunky gasped and grabbed me tightly as he came, but, like a drowning man who fights off his rescuer, he began to thrash around, bursting into tears and sobbing inconsolably. He wanted to be alone on his side of the bed and not be touched as he wept; he couldn't, or wouldn't, be comforted. But just as suddenly as he had reacted to his intense orgasm by weeping, he became his old self and apologized for his tearful outburst. That's the way he was, he told me. He feared his wedding night, not knowing how his fiancée was going to react to his peculiar behavior, though he had discussed it with her. He paused. And again time stood still, for two people so alone, whose love and souls merged into one, each trying to find himself and a little peace in the other, even if only for a moment.

I kissed him hard; he trembled and cried out as he came. Once more he began to weep and pushed me away. Then just as suddenly, he recovered and smiled apologetically. We talked for a few minutes. He got up, dressed quickly, hugged me, and kissed me on the neck, and that was that. He left. I haven't seen him in thirty-nine years. It would have been inappropriate to pursue him or to look him up years later. It was a few minutes I will never forget. Whatever happened to him— well, maybe one day, I will receive an e-mail message: Are you the guy I used to know?

– 13 –

465 Acres

Jay Quinn

Steve turned from his back to his side and reached through the cool expanse of sheets, seeking the warm, soft fullness of Janet's breasts. He could smell her in the bed, a feminine blend of sweetness over a hint of sweat and riper musk. His hand encountered not the hillocks he sought, but a smooth plain of flesh, blind of nipples and ridged with livid scars whose heat stung his fingertips. He heard Janet's soft welcoming moan. Ignoring the loss of her breasts, he moved his hand over the lush curve of her belly, anticipating the elastic of her panties. In response, she turned toward him.

He opened his eyes to find her sleepy smile. Steve saw her then, not looking at him with all the welcome of a summer morning's lover, but waxy, drawn, and silent. His bedroom became the viewing room at Turner's Funeral Home. He was surrounded by the sibilant sounds of sighs, sniffles, and quiet tears. Withdrawn, infinitely private, Janet's face reproached him in death for daring to violate her in her absence.

Steve jerked away from his dream. Fully awake and awash with horror and deep loss, he sat up and swung his thick legs over the side of the bed. The clock on the nightstand read five-fifteen. His dick, unheeding of reality, was knotted painfully in his boxer shorts. Ashamed and slightly angry, he spread his legs and adjusted himself resentfully. Then, defeated, he rested his elbows on his knees and his face in his hands.

"Two minutes," Steve thought. "I can do this for two minutes." He tried to recall Janet's living face, animated by the antics of the kids, singing in the choir at church, bent over a frying pan full of chicken. He couldn't. He looked for Robin's face, lost to him as well, but still alive. He saw him as he was at seventeen. The memories of Robin, old and sweet and bitter, never ceased to ease the fresher loss of Janet. His return to earlier pain made the present bearable. He looked at the clock; it said five-seventeen.

Steve stood and squared his broad shoulders. It was time to get on with it. Dispelling the fog of dreams with a mental recitation of the tasks ahead of him that day, he shaved, showered, and dressed. Before leaving the brightening bedroom, he stopped before the dresser to collect and gear himself with his change, wallet, keys, and pocket-knife. His watch was resting in front of the eight-by-ten Olan Mills portrait of Janet that they had taken right before she got pregnant with Bitsy. Steve peered at it as he pulled on his watch.

Janet's smile was oddly knowing in a way that had always made him uncomfortable. She knew. She'd always known. And her know-ing, in light of his coming meeting with Robin, made him feel guilty and dirty and sad. Abruptly, Steve pulled open his underwear drawer and shoved the neatly folded stacks of boxers and socks to one side. He picked up the portrait blindly and laid it, face down, in the drawer. He shoved the underwear and socks over it. Done. It was time to get on with it.

Opening the door of his bedroom, Steve heard Bitsy's soft scamper down the hall toward her bedroom. He caught a glimpse of her long, coltish legs flashing tan beneath her oversized T-shirt that she slept in. Her door closed behind her with a soft click.

Steve took three steps down the hall and stopped at Drew's bed-room door. Pushing it open gently with the flat of his hand, he peered into the northern darkness of Drew's room to find his son twisted in his sheets, one brawny leg thrust out bare, one thick arm over a pil-low, his broad, bare back too big for the twin bed, his face turned to-ward the wall. Drew always attacked sleep with the rough enthusiasm he directed at everything else. Steve allowed himself a smile before he said gruffly, "Boy, you better get up."

Drew mumbled in reply and rolled his shoulders more snugly into the mattress. "You better hear me, Drew. You got chores before you run off to the beach with your sorry-ass buddies." He watched his son raise his head and stare blankly toward the wall. "All right, Daddy. Five more minutes, okay?" Steve's head bobbed back in a silent chuckle. "All right, but don't make me have to call you again." Drew turned over on his back and kicked away the sheet. Steve caught a glimpse of his boy's morning erection straining against his jockey shorts. With a curious mixture of pride and shame, he closed the bedroom door and continued down the hall.

He could hear his mama moving around in the kitchen downstairs. The rich drifts of coffee and bacon scents had already made their way up. Steve stopped in front of Bitsy's door and rapped softly against its surface with his knuckles. "Girl, your horse ain't gonna feed itself," he said with the same gentle gruffness as he'd roused his son. When he received no response, he reached for the doorknob and found it locked to his twist. Bitsy had gotten mighty private lately, he noted. "Bitsy . . ."

"I'm up, Daddy," came her reply. "I'll be down in a minute." Steve peeked down at his feet. No gleam of light stole from beneath the door. "If you're up, why come I don't hear no Backstreet Boys?" Steve asked. In reply, he heard the unmistakable opening strains of the song he'd come to loathe. Satisfied, he turned and went downstairs.

"Morning, Mama," Steve said as he strode into the bright kitchen and seated himself at the head of the table opposite the window looking across the horse pasture to the Vincent place. He could still make out a light burning against the departing night. He was pleased. Robin was probably up and getting ready.

"Morning, son," his mama said as she set a cup of coffee in front of him. "You call the young'uns?" Steve grunted as he reached for the sugar bowl. Satisfied, she moved back toward the stove. Steve watched her as he stirred his coffee. She was still a handsome woman, his mama. Trim, impeccably groomed, and dressed in an oversized LaCoste shirt, neatly tucked into her jeans, her appearance belied her sixty years. She looked every inch the prosperous matriarch of what still passed for landed gentry in eastern North Carolina.

Briskly, she took up the last of the bacon from the blackened skillet, arranging it neatly on a platter alongside a small mountain of scrambled eggs. She turned the burner off underneath the skillet and moved back to the table with grace. Seating herself beside her son, she nodded toward the window. "The Vincent boy's up," she said.

Steve took a sip of his coffee to hide his annoyance. Setting his cup back in its saucer, he said, "Mama, Robin is forty, the same age as me."

His mama straightened herself in her chair and took a sip of her orange juice. "You know what I mean. There's no need to get snippy."

Steve turned his blue eyes to meet those of his mother. Ice to ice. He looked away first. Calmly, she continued, "A little bird told me Will Strickland took him out last night to the country club. Wining and dining. Will's been drooling over that 465 acres since before Robie Vincent passed." Steve looked at the platter of eggs and bacon but decided against it. He wasn't taking Robin Vincent to the country club, but he was taking him to the Bright Leaf Diner for breakfast. A self-assured man had an appetite. A nervous man picked at a plate of food.

"I'm not having no ticky-tacky subdivision full of Mexicans and white trash going up next to my land," his mother said and uncharacteristically took Steve's thick wrist in her hand. Squeezing it, she said heatedly, "Son, I don't care what it takes . . ."

Steve pulled away from his mama's painful grasp and raised his hand to rub his eyes. "Mama, this couldn't have come at no worse time. The hurricane last year damn near took us out. I don't know if I can beat Will Strickland's price."

Unabashed, his mama said, "Where there's a will, there's a way." Steve angrily pushed away his cup and saucer and leaned back in his chair, tipping it on its hind legs. He regarded his mama coldly. "Mama, what the hell do you want me to do? Corn's way down. We put all the lease land in soybeans, and that might bring some extra in, but . . ."

Sternly, his mama swept her eyes over him. "Sit in that chair like you got some sense." She waited until Steve brought all four chair legs to rest on the floor before she continued. "Janet's insurance money ain't doing nothing in the bank but growing that little piece of interest. Land's a better investment."

Steve pushed back from the table and stood up. He walked over to the sink and gripped its edge in frustration. When he could control his voice, he said, "Janet's money is for the young'uns' college." He heard his mama sigh. He knew she was simply gathering up for what would come next. He felt his neck tense waiting for it. Finally, she spat, "Community college is good enough for Drew. He's just gonna come back here and run this farm like you did and your daddy did and his daddy before that, on back for more than a hundred and fifty years. Bitsy's a girl. Ain't no use wasting money on no college for her. She's just gonna get married and go off the land to look after some other man's family."

Steve turned to stare at her defiantly. She lifted her chin and met his gaze head on. "Just look at the Vincents. Quakers. Always encouraging their young'uns to go off and go to school instead of staying home and making a decent life where they belong. Now it's come down to this: Old man Vincent dying over yonder with nobody to look after him after Sudie passed on. All their family strowed every which-a-ways. And nobody to come back and take care of business other than that boat-sick Robin. He won't never right, no way. I always thought he was half-damn crazy and too girlish to amount to anything."

"That's enough, Mama," Steve said. He glanced at the clock. It was time to go. He strode past the kitchen table toward the rack by the back door. Taking his John Deere cap from its peg, he pulled it on and tugged the brim low over his eyes. He heard his mother's chair legs scrape against the clean kitchen floor. Turning to leave, he heard her making her way toward him.

"Steve. You don't dismiss me," she said. He turned to look at her. His mama's lips turned up in a cruel little smile. Her eyes betrayed a smug little nugget of viciousness. Steve regretted having let it get to the point where she would pull out some painful bit of her long knowledge of him to use as a weapon. Looking at her, he knew it was too late. He felt his shoulders slump in defeat. She took two steps closer to him and hissed, "You liked Robin Vincent good enough at one time. I know how much he thought of you. Maybe you ought to take him down by the river and talk about old times."

If it had been any other human being breathing, Steve would have proceeded to beat the living shit out of them. But this was his mama. Without another word, he turned and walked out of the house, slamming the door behind him.

Steve started up his truck and tried to put his anger at his mama's insinuation behind him. She always knew just what to say to keep him in his place, to keep him under her heel, to remind him who was really the head of the family. It was as if she could look into his mind and see just what was nagging him and use that to her own advantage.

He looked guiltily across the flat pasture toward the Vincent place. Robin would be waiting for him now. He both dreaded and hoped that Robin would remember the same thing his mama had thrown up in his face just now. He couldn't know what Robin thought. He hadn't seen or spoken to him in twenty-two years. Not until two days ago at Robie Vincent's funeral. He backed up the truck and swung it around to head down the drive. There was no way of telling, but Steve figured he'd find out.

It took less than five minutes for Steve to drive out to the state road and then the mile and a half to the Vincent's drive. In that length of time, he ran over what he did know about Robin since he left home. He knew Robin had joined the Navy straight out of high school. Always boat crazy and in love with the sea, Robin had told him that's what he'd do, and that's what he did. His granddaddy used to mention he was off somewhere in the Pacific when Steve ran into him, but the older Robie Vincent got, the less you could count on anything he said being what he knew right then or what he knew from months or years before. Long before he died, he'd started calling Steve, Martin, thinking he was his daddy, who'd been dead for years.

Steve turned into the Vincent's drive, knowing little more about Robin and what he had been up to than he had for years. At the funeral, Robin had looked little different than he did as a kid. The sandy hair was close cropped and betrayed strands of silver. His face looked a bit sun-worn and weather-beaten, but no more so than Steve's own. Robin had stayed lean, where Steve had grown larger, not fat, but nobody would mistake him for a twenty-year-old. Robin, well, Steve supposed somebody could.

He stopped the truck in the yard by the front door. Immediately, he was surrounded by a pack of baying hounds. Robie Vincent had gotten more foolish over his deerhounds the older he got. He hadn't hunted deer for twenty years, but he kept breeding the dogs. Steve wondered what would become of them now. He'd always wanted a couple of his own, but his mama wouldn't hear of it.

"I got enough to do without looking after a bunch of foolish dogs that don't chop, don't hoe, and don't know when to get in out of the rain," she said time and again.

Steve heard a loud whistle and looked up to see Robin on the front porch. The sight of him filled Steve with a kind of blind joy. The dogs responded by clamoring up the steps and then into the house through the front door, which Robin held open for them. Amazed, Steve watched them disappear into the house. Robin closed the door behind him and walked to the truck without a backward glance. He opened the passenger door of the cab and swung in without as much as a pause.

Steve felt something old and hurt in him give way. The early morning summer light, Robin's cocky swagger, the recent harping of his mother, all made him feel more like he had on another Saturday morning left miles and years back up the road. It was like he was sixteen again and about to head out on a rare day of freedom. Too long bound by regret and responsibility, all it took was his old friend's familiar recklessness to loosen the constrictions he'd placed on himself.

Steve grinned at him and said, "Reckon them dogs'll tear the place up?"

Robin answered the grin with a tight smile and jerk of his chin. "Hoss, I don't give a damn if they do. You ready for some breakfast?" In reply, Steve threw the truck in reverse and then in a hard spin backward into the front yard. Robin produced a pack of cigarettes from his cutoff khakis and pounded them against the dash. "Tear it up," he said. Steve laughed out loud and hit the gas, throwing up a rooster tail of grass, dirt, and gravel as they tore off down the drive.

At the road, Steve barely hit the brakes before hitting the gas again. The back end of the truck fishtailed and the tires squealed. He left a good thirty feet of Firestone rubber on the blacktop as they headed out toward town. Robin tore the cellophane and foil off the cigarette pack and pulled one out. Wordlessly, he offered one to Steve, who shook his head no. Robin lit up and reached over, without leave, and started punching buttons on the radio. He hit the oldies station after a few tries. As the Marshall Tucker Band poured out of the speakers, Robin leaned back and smiled. "It's good to see you again, Ste."

Steve felt warmed by his use of the nickname. Nobody had called him that in a long time. "Good to see you; it's been awhile," he replied. Robin nodded and flicked his ashes out the window into the wind. "You still in the navy?"

Robin placed one ragged sneakered foot on the dash and said, "Retired, two months ago. Twenty-two years in, and now I'm set up."

"Retired? No shit? Where are you settling down, back out West?" Steve asked carefully.

Robin shook his head no and thumped his cigarette out the window. "Nah, I'm living back here, down in Atlantic Beach. Granddaddy left me the cottage too."

Steve considered this for a full minute without saying anything. Robin always did have the luck. Retired at forty, with a place at the beach. Finally, he asked, "So, you working anywhere?"

Robin nodded and turned in his seat to face him. Seemingly un-aware of the girlishness of the gesture, he folded one leg under him-self comfortably and said, "I'm building a head-boat out on Harker's Island. Steelhull. Forty-foot. I'm fitting her out as an excursion boat. Whale-watching tours and shit."

Steve looked over at Robin, amazed, but not. Ever since he was a kid, he had come up with the most outrageous schemes. This seemed as implausible and foolish as any of them. "What are you going to do come winter?" Steve asked soberly.

Robin laughed. "I got my harbor pilot's license. I can pick up some pay that way. I'm registered with the port already."

"You got the world by the ass then, don't you?" Steve said. It came out harsher than he intended.

"I suppose," Robin said, then asked, "Your mama still got you by yours?" Robin watched as Steve's knuckles turned white under their tan as he gripped the steering wheel silently. Steve stared straight ahead down the familiar road leading into town. Robin shifted back to sit with his feet down and his back properly off the door. Steve slowed the truck to a reasonable speed and said nothing until they pulled up in front of the Bright Leaf Diner.

"I'm sorry, Ste," Robin said quietly as Steve shut off the truck.

Steve opened his door and looked across at Robin briefly. "Forget it," he said as he got out of the truck and waited for Robin to do the same. When Robin got out and closed his door, Steve threw the lock and pushed ahead of him across the sidewalk into the diner.

The diner was generally deserted on Saturday mornings. The week-day patrons were mostly old men who clung to habit from long associ-ation. On Saturdays, they stayed home and slept late, gumming old dreams and chasing rabbits in their sleep. Robin and Steve took a prime booth by the front window. Robin looked out over the sad street. Many stores were dark; some were boarded up. A shadow passed over his face as he said, "The old town's looking bad, Ste. Hurricane?"

Steve shook his head. "River never made it up here, but it won't for lack of trying. Town's played out. Since the new mall came in, and Wal-Mart out on the bypass, nobody wants to come downtown no more."

Robin nodded. "Did the hurricane do much damage to your place? I heard the river flooding was bad between here and the coast."

Steve looked around nervously for Dordeen. Usually she'd have been in front of them with a pad in her paw ready to shoot the shit and take their order. She was nowhere to be seen. He looked back at Robin searchingly. He didn't want to open up any discussion of the river, but he thought he could at least nip any further talk of it in the bud. "Played hell down off your granddaddy's and my west end. It's a fucking mess. Downed trees, scrap, polluted as hell. Faircloth's hog lagoons got flooded out. Stank like shit for months. You'd get lost going back in there now." Robin looked at him with concern. "The State boys say it'll be years before it's safe to go swimming," Steve added casually.

Robin winced involuntarily and broke off his gaze to concentrate on lighting a cigarette. Steve felt a stab of guilt at bringing up the subject, and a simultaneous dark thrill. Obviously, Robin remembered everything he did. The shame and joy of it wasn't his alone. He searched Robin's face, the lingering prettiness echoed and enhanced the slightly wounded look in his eyes, but he said nothing in reply.

"Well, I'll be damned, is that you Robin Vincent?" The slightly shrill voice of Dordeen, the waitress and an old classmate, startled Steve. He sat back against the booth's slightly greasy vinyl back, suddenly aware he had leaned too far across the table in his search for Robin's reaction. "I thought you'd fell overboard out there in the Pacific somewhere."

"Hey, girl." Robin replied with a smile. "You're looking good these days."

Dordeen snorted and patted her ample hips. "Just more good-looking to hold onto these days. You ain't aged a bit, boy."

Robin laughed and said, "And you're still full of shit. But I mean that in a good way."

Dordeen laughed in reply, then said, "Sorry about your granddaddy. We sure are gonna miss him around here."

Robin nodded and picked up his menu. "You planning on taking over his place?" Dordeen asked. "It sure could use somebody to run it proper."

Robin put the menu down without opening it. "I'm a sailor, not a farmer. I'm selling it."

Dordeen glanced over at Steve and raised an eyebrow. Steve met her gaze impassively. "Will Strickland was in here the other day talking about how he'd love to get his hands on that 465 acres," she said.

Robin took a long hit off his cigarette and blew the smoke out through his nose. "Had dinner with him just last night," he replied.

Dordeen looked at Steve and laughed, "I bet that got your mama's panties in a wad. Everybody knows—"

"How about some fish and grits, Dordeen? I ain't had anything that good for breakfast since I left home," Robin interjected. Dordeen glanced at Steve apologetically.

"That sounds good to me too," Steve said.

Dordeen nodded. "Daddy got some fresh trout this morning. Eggs scrambled? Coffee?" Both men nodded. "Be about ten minutes, then," Dordeen said and walked away.

Robin ground out his cigarette. He looked at Steve expectantly, now that Dordeen was out of earshot. Steve pushed his cap back off his forehead and returned his gaze. Neither man said anything for a moment. Then Robin broke the awkward silence. "I was sorry to hear about Janet, Ste."

Steve made an economical gesture of dismissal and said, "Just one of those things, I reckon. Lord's will."

Robin nodded and said, "The kids are doing okay?"

Steve smiled. "Doing great. Drew's following in the old man's footsteps. He made first-string varsity football, this year. He's a hell of a softball player too. The church team is second in the regional tournament this summer."

Robin smiled and nodded happily. "How about your daughter?"

Steve laughed. "Horse-damn-crazy, just like her mama." He looked out the window and said, "I wish Janet could see her. She'd be mighty proud of both her young'uns." He turned back to watch Robin pick up a fork and trace a pattern in the paper napkin. "You ever get married?" Steve asked jovially, too jovially to his own ear.

Robin looked up through his lashes, another unguarded girlish gesture that caught Steve off guard. "Don't ask, don't tell," Robin replied evenly.

His response kicked Steve in the chest. He knew, for Robin, there had been others. The unexpected jealousy made him nauseous. He looked away and said, "Well, I guess that says it all, don't it?" Robin sighed and lit another cigarette. When Steve looked back across the table, Robin was staring at him. "What?" Steve demanded. Robin looked down at the ashtray and said nothing. They sat in silence while

Dordeen returned to serve them. They ate in silence and waited for her to collect their plates and freshen their coffee.

When Dordeen ambled back to the booth in the back of the diner, where she had a small television set tuned to an evangelical talk show, Steve reached in his back pocket and pulled out a neatly folded envelope. He slid it across the table to Robin, who opened it without looking at Steve. He read the contents, folded the single sheet of paper, and returned it to the envelope. Then, he glanced at his watch. "I need to be getting back. I got to see a man about a dog," Robin said. Steve nodded and called for Dordeen.

"It's ten even, Steve. Just leave it on the table," Dordeen replied. "I'm too damn tired to get up again, and it ain't even nine o'clock."

Both men stood, and Robin put the envelope in his back pocket while Steve reached in his own for his wallet. Robin reached in his own pocket and pulled out a wad of bills. "Keep it, Robin," Steve said. "This one's on me."

"Hey, Robin, don't be a stranger if the wind blows you this way again," Dordeen called from the back of the diner.

"I'll do that, girl." Robin replied. "But it'll have to be a damn hurricane to get me back in this neck of the woods." Dordeen laughed and waved them out.

Outside, Steve cocked his head and searched the sky. There wasn't a cloud in sight. The sun was already riding high, and the air was still as a cemetery on Christmas morning. "Thunderstorm come night," he thought. Robin was waiting by the truck's passenger door. "I wish the damn sky would crack open and swallow me up," Steve thought bitterly and unlocked the truck.

They didn't talk on the way back out of town. Steve was too proud to ask Robin's opinion of his offer, and Robin wasn't offering one. The hot wind from the open windows did little to dispel the tension in the cab. Nearing the Vincent's drive, Steve broke the silence by saying, "What are you gonna do with your granddaddy's dogs?"

Robin looked at his watch again. "Tommy Heath wants them. I suppose he'll be good to them. He's been as dog-crazy as granddaddy ever was, all his life."

Steve nodded as he turned into the Vincent's drive. "Tommy's a good ol' boy. He'll treat them durn dogs like family—hell, better than family."

Robin smiled and said, "Good. I couldn't stand to give them to somebody who'd beat them."

Steve pulled up in the drive by the front door. He put the truck in park and let it idle. "They're just dogs, Robin," he said evenly.

Robin turned in his seat and looked him in the eye. "Well, we all know how much loyalty you have, not to mention sentiment, when it comes to dogs or people," Robin replied.

Steve looked at him tiredly. He knew what Robin meant. "Them was old, long-ago times Robin. Let it go."

Robin looked out the window and raised himself slightly to retrieve the envelope from his back pocket. He laid it on the seat between them. "Tell me something, Ste. Tell me, honest to God. Was it what you wanted, or was it what your mama wanted?"

Steve hit his fist against the dashboard hard enough to crack it, but it held. Robin never flinched. "Robin, goddamn it, it was kid stuff, all those times, all those years. But we had to grow up. We weren't going to stay boys swimming in the river forever."

Robin looked at the envelope and then back at Steve. "You didn't answer my question. Was it what you wanted?" Steve hung his head and rubbed his eyes. He saw his mama, dappled by sunlight through the leaves and reflected river light. He saw his mama, slamming his bedroom door. He saw Robin, getting on the bus, alone, the bus that would take him to a future far away from this farm, this town, his arms, his heart.

"No. It wasn't what I wanted," he said, fighting back tears. "I loved you, Robin."

Robin sighed and put his hand on his shoulder. Squeezing it firmly, he said, "Well, then she fucked us both. I ain't never stopped loving you. At least she didn't kill that." Robin let go of his shoulder, opened the truck door, and got out.

"Robin, I wish I could take it back," Steve said desperately. Robin shut the door and said through the open window, "I accept your offer. Tell your mama the faggot thought it was worth 465 acres to hear her son say that." Steve watched him walk away, go up the steps, and enter the house. He never looked back.

Back home, Steve got out of the truck and walked tiredly into the kitchen. His mama sat at the table shelling peas. She looked up brightly as he hung his John Deere cap on its peg and said, "Well, that certainly didn't take long." Steve nodded and went to the refrigerator. He pulled out the water jug with his name on it and took long deep swallows of the cold to loosen the ache in his throat. "Close the refrigerator door. Are you trying to air-condition the whole house?" His mama said sharply.

Steve carefully snapped the small lid down on the cover of his water jug and replaced it on the refrigerator shelf. "Son, how long is it going to take you to learn that water jug won't fill itself. You'll be in here in an hour hunting some cold water and all that'll be left in that jug is that little dab of spit," his mama scolded. Without a word, Steve took the jug out of the refrigerator and walked over to the sink to refill it.

As he turned on the faucet and situated the jug so that the narrow stream ran precisely into the small opening of its lid, his mama said, "Well?"

Steve concentrated on watching the water move past the small precise tick marks engraved on the jug's plastic sides. "He accepted our offer," Steve said evenly.

"Which one?" His mama demanded.

Steve watched as the water neared the top of the jug and slowly turned off the faucet as it reached the bottom level of the lid. "The first one. The Vincent place is yours."

Steve didn't look at her as he returned the jug to its place in the refrigerator and closed the door. His mama laughed out loud. "Well, he's as crazy as I thought, then. I know Will Strickland offered him twice what we did. He could have made a killing off that 465 acres."

"He did." Steve said quietly and turned to go upstairs.

"Where are you going?" His mama asked. "I want to discuss what we're going to do with that property. Steve, don't you walk away from me while I'm talking to you. You act like you've lost all your sense . . . Steve?"

Steve walked heavily up the stairs. He walked down the hall, sun dappled by the morning light streaming through the leaves of the sycamores outside. Looking neither left nor right, he went in his bedroom and closed the door, locking it behind him. He opened the door of his closet and reached for his shotgun. He took it carefully and broke it open as he walked to the side of the bed nearest his nightstand. The two shells he kept there were precisely in their place, scented by cedar over the sharper smell of powder and steel shot.

He slowly sat down on the edge of the bed and placed the stock of the shotgun between his feet. With one shell in place, he fondled the other. The red shaft and bright brassy head reminded him of a young boy's dick—short, thick, and hard. He placed the end of the shell in his mouth and flicked the hard brass rim with his tongue. The dry red shaft dragged against his lips as he drew it slowly out and then hungrily pushed it back into his mouth. Spit-slicked and smooth, it soon glided between his lips with the ease he recalled from long ago.

Finally, tired of the ruse, tired of the game, Steve flung the shell away in disgust. His mind was made up. He removed the other shell from the barrel and placed it neatly back in his nightstand drawer. Rising, he closed the shotgun and strode over to return it to the corner of his closet. He pulled down a suitcase he hadn't used since his honeymoon and began to think of what he wanted to take.

His mama wasn't in the kitchen when Steve walked back downstairs. The large old house was silent and chill. He set down his suitcase and opened the refrigerator door. Taking his water jug from the shelf, he walked over to the sink and poured out its contents to the exact level he had intended to leave it at before. He returned it to its proper place, closed the door, picked up his suitcase, and walked to the back door.

As Steve took his John Deere cap off its peg and placed it on his head, he heard a soft sound he knew all too well. He tugged the brim low over his forehead as though anticipating a harsh glare. "Where do you think you're going?" his mother asked. Steve turned slowly to look at her. For the first time in his life, he realized that he was taller than she was.

"I'm going to Robin's, if he'll have me," he said quietly. He watched as his mother took two steps toward him and squared her shoulders. "Oh no you're not, not while I have breath in my body. You aren't going to shame this family. You ain't got so grown I can't fix things, like I did the last time."

Steve shook his head and laughed. "You can't do shit. What are you going to do, kill me? God knows you've been trying for years, and you know what, Mama? You almost succeeded. The hell with you, the hell with this farm and everything on it." Steve turned and picked up his suitcase.

"What about Drew and Bitsy? If you don't care nothing about me, after all I've done for you, what about your young'uns, your own flesh and blood?" his mother asked icily.

Steve reached for the doorknob and hesitated. He didn't know. He couldn't sort it out right then. He couldn't understand why it had to be all or nothing. He made his choice. "They'll either get over it, or they won't. That's up to them. Good-bye, Mama." Steve said, opened the door, and walked out.

"I'll make it so you never see them again. I'll make it so you never see another dime off this place," his mother shouted, following behind him as he walked down the steps.

Steve stopped and turned back to face her once more. "You try that, bitch, and I'll drag you into the county courthouse so fast it'll make your head spin. You forget, Daddy left this place to me. You ain't entitled to any more than what I'll let you have. And I swear before almighty God, you mess with me and I'll sell off acre by acre to fight you. Do you hear me, Mama?"

She stopped and gave him a look of such hatred, Steve wondered how hard she must have worked all those years to keep it hidden. Without another word, she reached out and slapped him hard against the mouth, turned, and strode back into the house.

Steve tossed his suitcase into the bed of his truck. He got in the cab and cranked her up. Once again, he looked across the pasture at the Vincent place. He pushed his cap up off his forehead, put the truck in gear, and headed out to the road, praying that Robin would have him.

– 14 –

Haunted by Home

Jeff Mann

In the summer of 1990, I visited Richmond, Virginia, for the first time. I strolled the Capitol grounds and toured the White House and the Museum of the Confederacy. At nearby Berkeley Plantation, I looked out over the James River, the manicured grounds bright with blooming crepe myrtle, and tried to imagine the strength it took for man or woman, Yankee or Confederate, to endure the Civil War. The setting inspired a poem, "Confederate Kiss," in which I tried to imagine the gay men who lived then, no doubt agonized by repression and guilt, the soldiers of the South who occasionally loved one another and who occasionally, despite great danger, expressed that love.

Confederate Kiss

Down by the broadening James, twilight
chants, thick with August. Along corridors
of crepe myrtle, boot heels are curving
toward the graveyard,

Confederate captain and sergeant meeting
among headstones, on furtive leave, in dusk.
Birds roost noisily in the great trees,

as we unbutton gray, in a chest-clink
of meeting medals, the drawl of love-words,
bearded kisses rough with bourbon and tobacco.

So the sourwood's bells peal open
to bee-probe and nestle, the honeydew
splits juicily beneath the knife.
The oyster, prized, spills its liquor,
rosy champagne escapes its cork.
So the long-reformed addict takes
his first guilty, euphoric moonshine sip,
petals leap past potential into advantage.

Far from the fires of approving hearth
or stoic bivouac, our tongues' deja vu,
our night-blooming surrenders.
The crepe myrtle's a brush of benediction,

as we cross swords, callused hands sliding through
moist nights of chest hair, fresh nakedness
lending purpose to Tidewater heat,
semen shuddering across vinca-dark grave sod.

On the way home, I visited Appomattox, standing by Surrender Triangle, where Lee's soldiers laid down their arms. And over the years since, I've wandered the March-misty fields of New Market Battlefield, strolled the Sunken Road at Fredericksburg, seen the sarvisberry bloom at Chancellorsville about the etched stone marking the spot where Stonewall Jackson fell. My vacations are often centered around touring spots important in Southern culture and history, such as Charleston, Savannah, and New Orleans, where I absorb the ambiance and batten on the local cuisine. Southerners are often accused of being nostalgic romantics, overly enamoured of the past, and I must confess to such a passion for history. Acquaintances sometimes roll their eyes with politically correct annoyance when they discover my admiration for Robert E. Lee or notice the Confederate flag sticker on my guitar case. I try to explain that Southern history sometimes feels like a throb beneath my breastbone; it often seems that personal and immediate. But most folk in mainstream American culture, absorbed in the difficulties of the present and transfixed by the possibilities of the future, rarely understand.

Pride in my heritage has been a long time coming. Ironically, it took leaving the South to make me realize that I was a Southerner. As a young gay man coming to terms with his sexuality in the small mountain town of Hinton, West Virginia, I detested the region as a homophobic and fundamentalist snakepit any gay person would be well rid of. It was only when I left my hometown to attend college in northern West Virginia, only a few miles from Pennsylvania, that I began to discover how much my early years in the rural South had shaped my identity, my values, my aesthetic sense. Slowly, I began to see more than the region's flaws. I began to recognize its fine points, and I began to feel a devotion to family and a deep attachment to the landscape. And the Southern qualities I displayed, occasionally mocked outside the region, became for me arousing attributes in other men: their good manners, their sense of honor, their hospitality, even their accents—all those characteristics traditionally found south of the Mason-Dixon line. As I fell in love with such men, I fell in love with the South, its history, its painful complexities and contradictions, all of which I began to locate within myself.

During those difficult high school years in Hinton, even as I feared the narrowmindedness and intolerant fundamentalism of the region, I greedily soaked in the details of the local mountain men, men who never knew I wanted them. Like most gay and lesbian youths who must conceal their desires to survive, I was a master of peripheral vision. Phys Ed, otherwise a torture for an uncoordinated scholar like me, became a source of erotic poetry. I ran my starved eyes like eager hands over the bodies of other boys in the showers. I relished shirts and skins in basketball, watching the muscles in Billy's chest bounce as he bounded down the court for a fine layup. One afternoon, we played tag football in the lawn by Hinton's war memorial. I still remember the diamond-shaped patch of sweaty dark hair between Alan's nipples when he stripped to the waist amidst a swarm of migrating monarch butterflies that suddenly encompassed us on their way south.

At this point in my adolescence, I was lucky enough to be surrounded by the Colony, a group of misfits who banded about Jo Davison, a freethinking lesbian biology teacher at Hinton High School. In this radical crew of liberal friends, I could come out at my own pace. One member of this circle proved to be an early sexual icon for me. Mike wasn't really an outcast like the rest of us; he was a handsome, popular football player, with a string of girlfriends. But some sense of right, combined with an innate streak of wildness, must have convinced him to become our protector. I was a quiet scholar; most of my other friends were lesbians. We were constantly threatened and mocked. Mike stood up for us. When his football team buddies insulted us, he brightly told them to kiss his lily-white ass. Most of us had not chosen our outcast status. He, on the other hand, had deliberately bucked convention and taken a stand, showing a rebellious courage I always admired—as I admired his looks.

Mike was the apotheosis of all that is best and most appealing in mountain men. He had dark hair, a catfish grin, cheek stubble that he occasionally grew out to a fine thick beard. In town, he strode around in ratty jeans, boots, and denim jackets. Occasionally, at Davison's farm, where the Colony hung out, he worked on his perpetually ailing old car. Invariably, he stripped to the waist, revealing big muscles and dark hair spreading lyrically over his chest and belly. When he crawled out from under the automobile innards, his shoulder or cheek would be streaked with oil. Yet, belying this deliciously rough exterior, he was bright, brave, and kind. An irresistible ideal, that combination of scruffy toughness and compassionate heart. Mike was both a role model and an early infatuation for me. One winter day, I hunted deer with him on the mountain above the Colony farmhouse. A baby butch, my lesbian friends would have called me, as I proudly sported my new Case XX knife, and though I prayed we would find no deer, I was very pleased that he'd invited me along. Spring of 1976, at a school camping trip to North Bend State Park, this mentor by the campfire ritualized our relationship by solemnly presenting me with my first bottle of alcohol. Annie Green Springs Berry Frost, I believe it was, appropriate syrup for a beginning drinker. I gulped it down my throat as if it were his masculinity I was consuming. That summer, around another campfire, in the midnight heat, he pulled off his shirt, and as I sipped whiskey with him, I watched the firelight and the shadow play across his muscles and thought about Plato, how beauty reveals God.

In high school, I was never brave enough to make a pass, but once I went to college and became a swaggering leatherstud-in-training, I planned to get Mike drunk on Canadian Lord Calvert, his favorite whiskey, and seduce him when we both returned to Hinton over Christmas break. He never showed up, and, true anticlimax, I haven't seen him since high school. I gather from town talk that he's been married and divorced, has traveled a lot, and rarely comes back to town. Nevertheless, over twenty years later, I'm grateful for the inspiration and the instruction. An early icon in my sexual and aesthetic development, he helped compose that constellation of elements that, for me, define the desirable.

In August 1977, I gladly escaped my hometown, drove to Morgantown, and began my undergraduate studies at West Virginia University. When, led by lesbian friends, I entered Morgantown gay life, I was unimpressed by the swirl of rampant queens at the Fox, the local gay bar. What I wanted, both in myself and in other men, was some version of Mike's mountain man masculinity, as well as that of literary figures I admired. In *Wuthering Heights,* Emily Brontë gave me Heathcliff, who raged and brooded with an intensity I envied. In *The Fancy Dancer* and *The Beauty Queen,* Patricia Nell Warren provided me leather-clad role models like Vidal Stump and Danny Blackburn, passionate and masculine gay men. I decided to become the kind of man I wanted. Armed with a sparse beard, new boots, old jeans, my first black leather jacket, and the volcanic testosterone of my late teens, I became a self-consciously butch barfly whose predatory hunger was only matched by his paralytic shyness. My friend Mona was wont to quip, "You only stop cruising when you're eating!" Not true. Even then, my restless eyes were picking out beard stubble, Levi jackets, and pectoral swell in the Mountainlair, WVU's student union. But my mother had raised me as a Southern gentleman, and approaching strangers for casual sex was not among the genteel skills she'd encouraged me to adopt. This inability to approach men, and so indulge my penchant for promiscuity, I see, in retrospect, probably saved my life, for my early cruising days were those years of the late 1970s, when AIDS was present but not yet identified.

Those years cruising the Fox and other gay bars, I was intelligent enough to notice that the men I found attractive, the men I emulated, were very like those Southern mountain men I'd grown up around, men I'd hungrily studied with that heady combination of fear and desire. This realization was strengthened when I decided to major in both English and forestry. My forestry classes in Percival Hall and my biology classes in Brooks Hall were abrim with incredibly sexy boys. Most of them were beefily muscular, used to the outdoors. They wore lumberjack boots, jeans, thermal undershirts, baseball caps, and flannel shirts. Most sported beards. The chest hair that had become a prime fetish of mine curled over their T-shirt tops, smoke from a mine fire. Most of them were much like me in their Southern upbringing: though they looked gruff, they were often soft-spoken and polite, with mountain or Deep South drawls. Having long ago learned protective coloration and, more recently, a butch, bar persona, I fit right in.

And eventually I began to feel less like a clever imposter and more like a man among men with whom I had much in common. I had always, on one level, been afraid of other men; all my earliest friends, in childhood and adolescence, had been women. My mother, grandmother, and sister had taken care of me. My father, influential as he'd been in many positive ways, was the disciplinarian and, thus, a source of fear. And, as I've said, I sensed that most of the guys I desired in high school would respond to my admiration with physical violence. But these forestry buddies I felt fairly easy around, though I certainly wasn't yet brave enough to come out to them. One of them, Randy, a married ex-firefighter with a full beard already silvering, became a regular companion. In classes, I studied the thick hair on his arms and fantasized about what he would look like after I pulled his shirt off. Amusingly, he thought I was a real stud because every time he saw me I was with a different woman. "Gigolo," he called me. What he didn't know was that all those women were lesbians.

Being surrounded by so many desirable forestry majors was both frustrating and inspiring. In botany lab, watching Dan spit snuff into a pop can and absent-mindedly give his pen head, I wondered if India ink could be any blacker than his beard. In mammalogy, I tried to memorize the imprint of Kevin's nipples against his WVU Forestry Club T-shirt (the motto on the back: "Foresters Do It in the Woods"). One blissful day, in aquatic seed plants, a course I took with most of my favorite lumberjack look-alikes, the professor took us out to Cheat Lake for lab. It was an early September afternoon, very hot, and the class ended up wading about in the mud looking for plants whose names I've long ago forgotten. What has not escaped my memory is all the doffed T-shirts. Every boy in the class stripped to the waist, including myself, a beginning weightlifter and thus a novice exhibitionist. There, briefly, were all the bare chests I'd fantasized about for semesters. An onanist's dream.

When classes ended, I spent the summers in my hometown. The erotic poetry I'd come to appreciate was everywhere. The country boys I lusted after rarely dispensed with their customary boots and jeans, even in hot weather, but they needed little excuse to peel off their shirts. This only deepened my obsession with bare chests. Shirtless men hoeing in their cornfields, shirtless men fishing hip-deep in the New River's jade currents, shirtless men driving dustily by in their pickup trucks. Studying the dark swirls of fur matting their torsos, I imagined the delicious contrast between soft hair over hard muscle. I remembered the woodlands I explored as a child, the rich moss I used to stroke, a carpet covering curves of sandstone.

One humid day, my hands actually got to clasp briefly what my eyes so constantly devoured. Down by the Bluestone Reservoir, I was drinking cheap beer and wine with a crew of college-age guys. That summer was especially hot, and we obliged the weather by stripping to torn jeans and cut-off shorts, sprawling on car hoods and occasionally taking a drunken dip in the reservoir's water. One boy had brought his motorcycle, and somehow I convinced him to take me for a ride, my first on the sort of bike all my leather-stud role models drove through novels and pornography. I don't remember his name, but I recall his gray half shirt, and how, when I climbed on behind him and he yelled "Hold on!" I could feel the sweaty hair on his belly. Frustrated and furtive, how grateful I was for an excuse to touch.

Ironically, despite my passion for all things Southern, despite the long yearning years of my youth lusting after mountain men, my relationships with other Southern men have, for the most part, been superficial or destructive. In the mid-1980s, I enjoyed an infrequent connection with a man in Beckley, West Virginia, not far from my hometown. Jim and I met one night in a huge, drafty building that once had been a Ponderosa, or some such steak house, and which for several months became a gay bar. Once again on the lookout for profound pecs, I noticed his nicely trimmed beard, the curve of his chest beneath a tight T-shirt. In the parking lot, amidst chittering dry December weeds and dervishing snow, we kissed, digging through layers of winter wear and down to skin, catching curls of chest hair between our eager fingers.

There was to be no real romantic attachment; we were more like buddies who included sex among the several recreational activities we shared. We jogged together, hit the Beckley YMCA to lift weights, admired each other's exercise-pumped biceps, then slipped into the whirlpool bath to toe each other beneath conveniently concealing bubble-swirl. Once home, we experimented with kink, took turns on top, then, like a couple of college boys, ordered pizza, drank cheap beer, and watched junk TV.

Two of Jim's attributes were distinctly Southern, one of them appealing, one of them not. He had a strong West Virginia mountain accent, which I found pretty sexy. One day, we met for lunch at a Chinese restaurant in Beckley. When he went to the restroom, he returned almost instantly, brow furrowed with consternation, and informed me that a "warsp" had menaced him. When the waitress was informed of this problem, things got confused. She clearly could speak little English, but she listened intently, shaking her head and repeating shrilly, "Warsp? Warsp?!" Eventually he gave up and returned to his chow mein, leaving the vicious warsp to live another day.

Like many Appalachians, Jim was also very devoted to his family. This is the kind way to put it. He was terrorized by his mother, to be more honest. She would call in the morning to see if he was up and at evening's end to make sure he was ready for bed. Jim was totally closeted, playing piano Sunday mornings for a nearby Baptist church and dating women for appearances' sake, so he lived with the fear that his parents, his neighbors, and his church's congregation would discover the truth about his sexuality. I was his "Off Night Backstreet," to use a Joni Mitchell song title. This was fine with me. After all, our relationship wasn't about love; it was about infrequent and mutually beneficial erotic workouts. And sneaking around could be exciting.

But one afternoon the secrecy got absurdly out of hand. I was visiting for a few days, but Jim had forbidden me to leave the house, despite the warm weather. If the neighbors saw me, what would they think? Shrieking and mincing aren't my style, so I thought he was being a bit paranoid, but I acquiesced. Clad rather tastily in nothing but a pair of cutoff shorts, he began washing his car in the hot sun of the front lawn. I wanted to peel down, too, and join him, for two sweaty shirtless butch boys lathering metal and splashing about together sounded like pleasant foreplay, but I obeyed his dictate. I mixed myself a scotch and 7-Up and began playing his piano.

Then the phone rang. Of course, Jim's Dirty Little Secret couldn't answer, so I ignored it. A few minutes later the phone rang again. Again I ignored it. Five minutes later Jim tore through the front door in a panic. His mother, having called twice without getting an answer, had decided to drive over to see what the problem was. "Jesus, Gawd, hide!" he howled.

I seized my drink and my piano music, rushed to the bedroom for my suitcase, descended to the basement rec room, then with the desperation of a cornered varmint looked around for a place to hide from this as-yet-unmet maternal harpy. The furnace room. I dove inside like a vampire at dawn and pulled the door shut behind me. For the next fifteen minutes, thankful that the dark little space was at least roomier than a closet, I sat on my suitcase, sipped my drink, and listened to their voices upstairs. His mother at this distance sounded like the teacher in Peanuts television specials. I could laugh at all this because my relationship with Jim was casual. As a mountain boy, I already had a taste for storytelling, and as I sat snickering on my suitcase, I knew I'd be telling this one for a long time.

There was nothing casual or amusing about my next affair with a Southern man. Or, I should say, with a man brought up in the South. I didn't realize there was a difference until I met Thomas. Though he'd grown up in Powhatan, Virginia, his parents were from New England. He lacked an accent, made fun of mine, had no respect for Southern culture, and proudly informed me that he'd never, ever eaten grits. At the same time, I began to realize that, even as he mocked me, he found my mountain man look appealing. He seemed reluctantly to admire my leather jacket, my harness-strap boots and muscle shirts, my black beard already stippling with silver. He even confessed to me that in his teenage fantasies, he'd often been tied up and abducted by a wild and handsome hillbilly.

I was introduced to him by a mutual friend in the War Memorial Gym at Virginia Tech, where I've taught since 1989. He rose from the weight bench and shook my hand. I was impressed: he was 5'8'' to my 6'1'', yet he bench-pressed twice as much as I. His muscles and his mustache fascinated me, but he had a longtime lover, he soon informed me.

Nevertheless, we shared a mutual interest in neopaganism and the occult, so we began meeting for coffee. Thomas was intelligent, witty, opinionated, and he exuded erotic charisma. I admired his knowledge as well as his pecs. Sexual tension quickly mounted between us, but I still couldn't believe a man I thought so desirable—he practically embodied Eros—would be interested in me. Then, one April evening, Thomas, his lover Jon, and I attended an Allen Ginsberg reading in Radford, Virginia. Through a stroke of luck, Jon knew the woman who was escorting Ginsberg around, so after the reading, we joined a small group accompanying the famous man to BT's, a local hangout. Pitchers of Killian's were quaffed, Jon listened fascinatedly to Ginsberg, Ginsberg flirted with the only straight man at the table, and Thomas and I talked about Aleister Crowley, the infamous English magus, and his theories about sex magic. Somehow, my feet got tangled with Thomas's, and soon we were playing footsie beneath the table like furtive teenagers.

A week later, we met in an acquaintance's borrowed A-frame in the woods near town. As I peeled off his shirt and ran my hands over his gym-hard chest, shoulders, and arms, and I pressed my face into the thick dark hair of his torso and belly, I thought of the Giant of Cerne Abbas, that great hill carving in southern England, a Celtic Hercules brandishing a club and an erect penis. I thought of Pan, Herne, and Cernunnos, the furry, horned fertility gods of ancient Europe. I thought of theophany, gods manifesting in human form. What I found most beautiful I held in my arms.

It was hard to let go, time and time again. It was hard to make love to an adulterer's schedule, to make love with our wristwatches on. It was hard to get to know Thomas's lover Jon, to deceive him, and eventually to love and respect him too. But at last I was living my version of *Wuthering Heights*. I was writing poetry like a madman.

Of course it ended badly. After a spring and summer of this drama, they moved that autumn to New England for employment. I visited once. When Jon went to work at Borders, Thomas and I, separated for months, tore off each other's clothes and filled our mouths with the body's bread. Then, stroking his beard stubble, the night-dark fur about his nipples, I told him that I couldn't continue our affair: it was too agonizing. He went into one room, to meditate, he said, and I went into the other. Dusk fell; Framingham 5 p.m. traffic droned by. I lay on the couch and listened to late-winter wind slam the apartment windows. Then Jon came home. We ordered pizza, we drank Rolling Rock beer, and we watched a movie. They went to bed together; I slept on the couch. The next morning, I kissed both of their brows and drove back to Virginia.

For three years, there was no contact. Then a card came with familiar handwriting and a Falls Church, Virginia, address. I wanted to see if
my feelings for him had ever been real, or simply a crazed mythology I'd
invented to make my world more like the Brontës'. A few stolen weekends together when his lover was out of town, that beautiful body once
again arching beneath my lips and hands. Then violent arguments, tears
on both sides. Via e-mail, a final and bitter break. After all my devoted
anguish, he left Jon for another man, not me. Months later, a mutual acquaintance told me that Thomas and Jon had reconciled and moved to
California. How strange it was, I thought, that I could still love so insanely a man I could never forgive. And how ironic that my ardor, desperate to escape isolation, had only deepened it.

Another painful and misplaced passion dwindling into history, and
Emily Brontë appropriately provides the postscript. One summer in
the mid-1990s, I served as assistant for an older professor who was
conducting a Study Abroad program for Virginia Tech. As our bus
slipped through the English countryside, I overheard Mr. Owen dis-
cussing *Wuthering Heights* with a student. "Well, literature often
takes human life and exaggerates it to an extreme for dramatic effect," he opined. "As for Catherine and Heathcliff, no one feels that
intensely." The student nodded, made safe by that assumption. I
smiled and returned to window gazing, watching the hedgerows and
church spires materialize and vanish, the fog roll in from the sea.

For a long time after this, unable to trust my own heart, I side-
stepped emotional risks through more recreational sex. Yankee boys
or Southerners, I didn't care, as long as they were reasonably masculine men, preferably sporting facial hair and memorably muscled
hairy chests. Leather bars and Bear gatherings, I'd long ago discovered, tended to be populated with the kind of men I liked, the kind of
men who liked me. One friend joked that all the guys I drooled over
looked like they stepped out of a lumberjack camp.

For many lonely years, meeting no one who inspired any depth of
feeling in me, I wondered if I'd have to leave the South to find a mate.
Dealing with the urban annoyances of DC, the nearest major city, was
something I was less and less willing to do; I hated the crowds, the
noise, and the traffic. But for a while it seemed that I'd have to choose
between my love of the South, its small towns, its countryside, and
my love of men. I thought I knew the kind of man I wanted: someone

displaying that slightly rough mountain man appearance I loved, but with intellectual and cultural interests. The only man I knew like that was me.

Lesbian friends in long-term relationships have told me for decades that you rarely end up with Your Type. In my case they were right. And luckily, with experience, one's Type tends to broaden over the years anyway; one begins to see beauty in a wider variety of men. Recently, my twenty years of bad luck changed; I discovered that, against all evidence, I could love a man who was good for me. Other than being blessed with a fine crop of body hair, my lover John is nothing like the mountain man sexual icon I've pursued for years. His family's roots are in New England. He is well-dressed, poised, radiating cultured good taste. He is controlled, while I am passionate. He is calm and logical, while I am often irrational, impatient, and hot-tempered. Somehow he tolerates all that wildfire. He grounds me, keeps me sane, like a levee holding back erratic floodwaters. He provides me with the first love I've ever felt that is healthy, not insanely histrionic and self-destructive. After several years together, I'm beginning to think that one Southerner in the household is enough.

The other day I asked him what it was like to be involved with a Southern man, what regional qualities of mine had an impact on our relationship. His first response was "Fried cabbage!" Which is to say, we're food enthusiasts who often cook for each other, and I've introduced him to any number of specifically Southern and Appalachian dishes. He'd never heard of fried cabbage until the recent millennium celebrations, when I explained to him that West Virginians always serve that dish on New Year's Day. He's also discovered that bacon grease must be saved to flavor collards, kale, and other greens, that sausage gravy and biscuits is a tasty, if heavy, way to start a weekend morning, that cornbread baked in a cast-iron skillet is the proper accompaniment to brown beans. He's sampled chow chow, ramps, half runners, creecy greens, dilly beans, wilted lettuce, and he's enjoyed them all, as well as the many summer vegetables from my father's carefully tended gardens.

Other Southern mountain attributes of mine he mentioned are unusually strong connections to family and place, qualities many have noted as being characteristic of Appalachians. Despite the discomfort and displacement I felt as a gay teenager in small-town Hinton, now I return there as often as I can. I never grow tired of the beauty of the Appalachian mountains, the epic of the shifting seasons, and Hinton is dramatically situated at the base of great hills by the New River. I feel more at home there than anywhere, and my mental balance is strengthened by regular visits. Seeing my family helps put things in perspective, as do walks in our pastures and woodlands, among the stones of our family graveyard.

John also mentioned a traditional and compulsory politeness he's noticed in me, as well as in other Southerners. No surprise here either. But, as he gently pointed out, this concern with manners often becomes a kind of Janus-headed two-facedness: sweet in your presence, bitchy behind your back. I'm reminded of Florence King's classic lines in her wonderful work *Southern Ladies and Gentlemen:* "Oh, I just hate and despise that Ginny. She's just so—Why, Ginny! Of all people! We were just talkin' about you. Come right in, 'deed we're so glad to see you, darlin'."

I'm guessing that John's too kind to point out other regional traits of mine that are less attractive. I'm a rampant snob; it's a snobbery that's too complex to easily classify, but it's a dominant element of my psyche. I'm prickly as hell, quick to anger. When, a few years ago, I saw an article in a newspaper announcing that researchers had discovered that Southern men are easily offended, I laughed out loud. As if this were news! Like most rural and small-town folk, I have a huge sense of personal space and in cities am constantly flooded with the urge to backhand urban dwellers who invade my territory. Finally, I possess an enormous pride, an overinflated sense of honor that, needless to say, only fuels the hot temper.

And, in an increasingly impolite and fast-paced world, my outrage over bad manners has become a crippling handicap. These days, most people do not share the old-fashioned Southern values I was brought up to believe in. An unabashed ethnocentrist, I regard such folk as rude and ill-bred annoyances, products of inexcusably incompetent child rearing. They are brusque; they are surly; they thoughtlessly impinge on the peace and quiet of others. So the mother brings her screaming infant to the movie theater; parents let their children run howling down the aisle of the airplane; restaurant patrons speak so loudly it interferes with conversations at adjoining tables. Fools with insufferable taste in music, the sort of vulgar bass-beat mimicking the copulation of beasts, drive their cars down midnight residential streets, the volume so loud that roused sleepers can feel the throb in their guts. ("Deaf by thirty," I snarl, but that's cold comfort, a vengeance not immediate enough to satisfy.) How difficult it must be for my lover to live with the rage I daily display over the world's worsening incivilities. No wonder I've developed from a young gay man hot to experience life in the Big City to a middle-aged gay man who cherishes his infrequent returns to hometown comfort, his escapes into the Appalachian countryside. Well on my way to becoming an eccentric recluse.

Let me finish with one last trait common to most self-aware Southerners, and, for that matter, to anyone thoughtful. *"There's always someone haunting someone,"* Carly Simon sings. For men like me, being Southern is the form our haunting takes, always attended by the ghosts of regional, family, and personal history. Memory can be a painful burden. But how uninteresting, how shallow are the unhaunted ones, with as little character as a freshly built house. I am haunted by those guns relinquished at Appomattox, the curving railroad tracks at Matewan, barges pushing snow-striped coal down the Kanawha River. I am haunted by my grandmother's grave plaque, my aunt's epitaph, my mother's ashes and abandoned clothes. I am haunted by memories of the men I've loved: the beards I've nuzzled, the chest hair I've stroked, the muscles and mortalities I've run my reverent lips along. Those beauties, like the landscape, have allowed me some sense of the sacred.

In *Giovanni's Room,* James Baldwin writes that "perhaps home is not a place but simply an irrevocable condition." It may be, as he suggests, that history is inescapable, defining us the way rain carves sandstone outcrops and wind flags mountain spruce. But the sorrows and anguish of the Southern past, the gay past—pains survived, losses endured—can enrich. The damaged who learn from their damage find wisdom and depth in their wounds. True of the South, and certainly true of those of us who live and die always haunted by home.

ABOUT THE EDITOR

Jay Quinn is a native of coastal North Carolina. He is the author of *The Mentor: A Memoir of Friendship and Gay Identity.* His novel, *Metes and Bounds,* will be published by Southern Tier Editions in 2001. A critic and regular columnist for *Lambda Book Report,* he lives and works in South Florida.

CONTRIBUTORS

Andrew W. M. Beierle is an Atlanta-based writer and editor who spent his formative years in Central Florida. This story is adapted from his unpublished debut novel, *The Winter of Our Discothèque.*

Jameson Currier is the author of a collection of short stories, *Dancing on the Moon,* and a novel, *Where the Rainbow Ends.* A native of Marietta, Georgia, he attended Emory University and currently resides in Manhattan.

Dayton Estes is a North Carolinian by birth. He taught German and German Literature and Philology for twenty-eight years at Pfeiffer College in Misenheimer, North Carolina. He is retired and lives in Oak Island, North Carolina.

Walter Holland, PhD, is the author of *A Journal of the Plague Years: Poems 1979-1992,* and a novel, *The March.* He has written book reviews for *Lambda Book Report.* His short stories have been published in *Art and Understanding* as well as the *Harrington Gay Men's Fiction Quarterly.* His poetry credits include *Art and Understanding, Barrow Street, Bay Windows, Body Positive, Christopher Street, Found Object, Men's Style, Phoebe, Poets for Life: 76 Poets Respond to AIDS, The George Mason Review, The Harvard Gay & Lesbian Review, The James White Review, The Literary Review, The Piedmont Literary Review,* and *Provincetown Magazine.* He also has been featured on B.B.C. Radio and his poetry has appeared in the British anthology of AIDS poetry, *Jugular Defences: An AIDS Anthology,* and *The Columbia Anthology of Gay Literature.*

Daniel M. Jaffe is currently editing an international anthology of Jewish-themed fabulist fiction. His translation of the Russian-Israeli novel *Here Comes the Messiah!* by Dina Rubina is forthcoming. Dozens of Dan's short stories and essays have appeared in such publications as *The James White Review, Christopher Street, The Greensboro Review, The Chattahoochee Review,* and *Green Mountains Review.* Dan is the recipient of a Massachusetts Cultural Council Professional Development Grant. He teaches fiction writing at UCLA Extension (online) and the Cambridge Center for Adult Education.

Robin Lippincott was born and raised in Central Florida. He is the author of three books: *The Real, True Angel,* a collection of short stories (1996); *Mr. Dalloway,* a novel (1999); and *Our Arcadia,* a novel, to be published in April 2001. He is currently at work on a novel set in the South titled *Tales of a Kudzu Warrior.*

Thomas L. Long is Associate Professor of English at Thomas Nelson Community College and editor of the *Harrington Gay Men's Fiction Quarterly.* His fiction has been published in *Blithe House Quarterly.* "Revelation" is part of a novel in progress, whose working title is *High Mass, Low Life.*

Jeff Mann grew up in southwest Virginia and southern West Virginia. He has published in *The Laurel Review, Antietam Review, Poet Lore, Appalachian Heritage, The Hampden-Sydney Poetry Review, Spoon River Poetry Review,* and *Prairie Schooner.* His collection, *Bliss,* won the 1997 Stonewall Chapbook Competition and was published in 1998. *Mountain Fireflies,* which won the 1999 Poetic Matrix Chapbook Series, and *Flint Shards from Sussex,* which won the First Annual Gival Press Chapbook Competition, were published in 2000. He teaches Appalachian Studies and Creative Writing at Virginia Tech.

J. E. Robinson's poems and short stories have appeared in *Galley Sail Review, Great Lawn, The Harrisburg Review, Janus, Men on Men 6, New Directions, Other Countries, Poetry Motel, re: Verse!, Unknowns, Voices from the Edge,* and *The Wittenberg Review.* He has contributed to *Gay and Lesbian Literature,* Volume Two; *Lambda Book Report;* and *Lavender Salon Reader.* He is working on a novel, *Waiting on Eurydice.*

George Singer is a playwright with an MFA from the Iowa Playwrights Workshop. His plays have been performed in London; Washington, DC; San Francisco; and New York. He also wrote the screenplay for the short film *Assassination,* which won second place in the International Lesbian and Gay Film Festival in San Francisco. "The Preacher's Son" is his first published story.

Dan Stone's poetry and fiction have appeared in *Bay Windows, Mostly Maine, Chiron Review, Queer Poets Journal, Brave New Tick,* and in *Gents, Bad Boys, and Barbarians: New Gay Male Poetry.* He's a recovering Christian and part-time freelance writer who lives in Washington, DC.

John Trumbo is a marketing copywriter and fiction writer in Washington, DC, whose work has appeared in *Christopher Street.*

Ed Wolf is originally from New York City and lived in North Miami, Florida, as a youth. His work has appeared in *Kaleidoscope, Transfer 35 and 36, The Bay Area Reporter, The National Library of Poetry: At Day's End, Beyond Definition: New Writing from Gay and Lesbian San Francisco, Art and Understanding, Poetry Motel, Christopher Street, The James White Review,* and *Prentice Hall's Discovering Literature.* He has been nominated for the Pushcart Prize and has recently completed a book of poetry and prose about the AIDS epidemic titled, *One Life, One Death.*

Order Your Own Copy of
This Important Book for Your Personal Library!

REBEL YELL
Stories by Contemporary Southern Gay Authors

_____ in hardbound at $34.95 (ISBN: 1-56023-160-2)
_____ in softbound at $14.95 (ISBN: 1-56023-161-0)

COST OF BOOKS_____	❏ **BILL ME LATER:** ($5 service charge will be added)
	(Bill-me option is good on US/Canada/Mexico orders only; not good to jobbers, wholesalers, or subscription agencies.)
OUTSIDE USA/CANADA/ MEXICO: ADD 20%_____	
	❏ Check here if billing address is different from shipping address and attach purchase order and billing address information.
POSTAGE & HANDLING_____	
(US: $4.00 for first book & $1.50 for each additional book)	
Outside US: $5.00 for first book & $2.00 for each additional book)	Signature_____
SUBTOTAL_____	❏ **PAYMENT ENCLOSED:** $_____
in Canada: add 7% GST____	❏ **PLEASE CHARGE TO MY CREDIT CARD.**
STATE TAX____	❏ Visa ❏ MasterCard ❏ AmEx ❏ Discover
(NY, OH & MIN residents, please add appropriate local sales tax)	❏ Diner's Club ❏ Eurocard ❏ JCB
FINAL TOTAL____	Account # _____
(If paying in Canadian funds, convert using the current exchange rate, UNESCO coupons welcome.)	Exp. Date_____
	Signature_____

Prices in US dollars and subject to change without notice.

NAME_____

INSTITUTION_____

ADDRESS_____

CITY_____

STATE/ZIP_____

COUNTRY_____ COUNTY (NY residents only)_____

TEL_____ FAX_____

E-MAIL_____

May we use your e-mail address for confirmations and other types of information? ❏ Yes ❏ No
We appreciate receiving your e-mail address and fax number. Haworth would like to e-mail or fax special
discount offers to you, as a preferred customer. **We will never share, rent, or exchange your e-mail address
or fax number.** We regard such actions as an invasion of your privacy.

Order From Your Local Bookstore or Directly From
The Haworth Press, Inc.
10 Alice Street, Binghamton, New York 13904-1580 • USA
TELEPHONE: 1-800-HAWORTH (1-800-429-6784) / Outside US/Canada: (607) 722-5857
FAX: 1-800-895-0582 / Outside US/Canada: (607) 722-6362
E-mail: getinfo@haworthpressinc.com
PLEASE PHOTOCOPY THIS FORM FOR YOUR PERSONAL USE.
www.HaworthPress.com

BOF00